THE GOOLZ NEXT DOOR

A BAD NIGHT FOR BULLIES

THE COOLZ NEXT DOORZ

BOOK I

A BAD NIGHT FOR BULLIES

GARY GHISLAIN

BOYDS MILLS PRESS
AN IMPRINT OF HIGHLIGHTS
Honesdale, Pennsylvania

For information about permission to reproduce
selections from this book, please contact
permissions@highlights.com.

Boyds Mills Press
An Imprint of Highlights
815 Church Street
Honesdale, Pennsylvania 18431
Printed in the United States of America

ISBN: 978-1-62979-677-2
eBook ISBN: 978-1-68437-135-8
Library of Congress Control Number: 201794846

First edition

10 9 8 7 6 5 4 3 2 1
Designed by Barbara Grzeslo
The titles are set in Bourton Base Drop.
The text is set in Bembo.

To Ilo, Sisko, and Elsa,
my stars quivering above.

"O people from the stars!
I am a man by a river, gazing up.
And how these stars quiver above.
How these lights reach farther than
I can see. And what of hidden
things?"

The Egyptian Book of the Dead

1

ACROSS
THE
BRIDGE

My mum had been obsessing over Frank Goolz for weeks.

"Come and meet him with me!" she called from downstairs. "I heard he's a lovely man. Weird as a blue carrot, but still a nice chap."

"Heard where?" I yelled from my room, where I was sitting in front of my computer, Googling Frank Goolz and being even more obsessive than she was.

"Heard *everywhere*," she responded.

I had a picture of him open on my computer screen. It was from an interview he'd done with the *New York Times*. He looked nice and approachable for such a literary superstar—a middle-aged man with messy salt-

and-pepper hair, smiling gently and staring straight at me with intense blue eyes.

"Harold!" Mum squealed. "I made a cheesecake. Please come along."

I pushed away from my desk and made a cool spin on my back wheels before going to the stairs.

Mum was in the hall downstairs, cheesecake in hand. She was wearing her bright yellow raincoat and knee-high yellow rubber boots. She looked like a giant canary.

"You're going to see him dressed like *that*?" I asked.

"Well, you're still in your pajamas, you silly sausage," she pointed out.

"My dear mum, I decline your invitation," I said, mimicking her British accent. My own accent had Americanized perfectly in the years since we moved from England to Maine. "I send you and your cake as my ambassadors. Welcome him to our shores and remind him to stay away from the quicksand at low tide."

Mum and I were binge readers and our house was an ever-growing library. When we heard that Frank Goolz had bought the house next door, we went to our favorite bookstore in Bay Harbor and ordered a dozen of his horror novels. We devoured them as they came in, lying side by side on the sofa and reading the scariest bits aloud.

"Why won't you come? You love his books," she said, opening the front door. "Just come and tell him that. He'll be delighted."

"Nah, I'm fine." I pressed the button and played with the stair lift, sending it down and bringing it back up. I was *dying* to meet him and tell him I loved his novels. They were great stories of creepy old mansions, eerie attics, cursed Voodoo dolls, and murderous mummies in exotic places. They were scary and exciting and full of the type of adventure I dreamed I could be a part of. But that's exactly why I was resisting meeting him in real life. He was an adventurer. A traveler. A mystery hunter. A man of a thousand legends and almost as many books. And I was just a boy in a wheelchair.

* * *

Mum finally gave up and left the house with her cheesecake. I went back to my room and up to the window, where I had a perfect view of the house next door. I looked down and saw Mum crossing the small bridge across the stream that separated our properties. I don't know who built that bridge or why. The stream is so tiny you could just jump across. I mean *I* couldn't jump, but a lot of people could.

11

Mum knocked on the door and waited a long time for him to answer. She was about to knock again when Frank Goolz finally opened the door.

I lifted myself up in my chair to get a better look. He was dressed elegantly in a white shirt and black trousers, but I could see he was barefoot. He looked exactly like the pictures I'd found online.

He grabbed the cheesecake as Mum babbled away. She couldn't stop talking when she was nervous. I smiled as I watched her blushing as red as poppies in spring. And then I stopped smiling because I realized I was being observed too.

Two girls were in Frank Goolz's yard, looking up at me. The smaller one waved. It took me a couple seconds to wave back. The older one said something I couldn't hear and smiled at me. She was about my age, or maybe a little older—like thirteen, tops.

I shoved away from the window fast, face burning. My Google search hadn't told me that Frank Goolz came with two girls (and possibly a wife).

I sat in the middle of my room for a while, feeling incredibly silly. Finally I decided to change out of my pajamas.

I threw my clothes on my bed, hoisted myself up, and snaked my legs into my jeans. Once I was dressed,

I went back to the stairs and pressed the button for the lift. I slid my bum into it and pushed my chair down the stairs, letting it fall freely. I did that only when Mum wasn't home. When she was around, she either carried the chair down for me or forced me to hold on to it while going down on the lift. She was sure that I was eventually going to break the chair by throwing it down the stairs. She also complained that I was scratching up the steps and walls. Plus, sometimes my chair landed on its wheels and rolled out of reach, trapping me on the lift. Which was exactly what happened that time.

Mum came back in the house, and saw me stranded. I almost wished that I'd tried to slide off the lift and crawl to my chair, but the last time I did that, I'd crash-landed right on my face.

I unbuckled the seatbelt from the lift. "The chair, please," I said.

It took her a couple seconds to decide not to lecture me.

"That was fast," I said, sliding into my wheelchair. "Didn't he invite you in to share some of your cake?"

Her cheeks were still glowing from her encounter with our famous new neighbor.

"He said he was busy with something, the ungrateful goose," she said. "Did you know he has two daughters?"

"No, I didn't." I pulled my jacket off its hook in the hall, put it on, and raced out like the house was on fire.

• • •

It's hard work pretending not to be interested in something you're really interested in. Mum had installed concrete paths all over our yard so I could move around. One path led to the bridge, but that was pretty useless, because on the other side there was nothing but sand and plants, and sand isn't really my thing. I pretended I wasn't interested in the Goolz's new home and went in the other direction, but I took a peek sideways to see if the girls were still in their yard. They were gone.

I climbed the little hill to our shed and stopped short right in front of it, where I could see all the way to the water. It was low tide, and the ocean was far away. The girls were on the beach, looking down at something and scratching the wet sand with a stick. After a minute they stood and walked along the beach toward the pier. I called for Mum, and she popped her head out the kitchen window.

"Do we need bread?" I asked casually.

"Not really," she said. And then she thought about it. "Do you want to get bread? Fresh bread's always nice."

The bakery in Bay Harbor and its fresh whole-nut

bread was one of our favorite things. That, and a stroll to the bookstore.

"I can get fresh bread," I said, like I was doing her a favor.

She came out with her purse. "Do you want me to come with you?"

I took a few dollars and told her I was fine. The Goolz girls were already almost to the boardwalk.

I started wheeling at top speed and reached the road in no time. I saw Frank Goolz through his window and waved, but he didn't wave back. I think he was eating some of the cheesecake.

"Ungrateful goose," I muttered.

2

FRESH BREAD'S ALWAYS NICE

I was a cool kid. I dressed OK. I had true grit and tons of attitude. If I were standing up, walking like everybody else, no one would ever pick on me. But in my wheelchair, I was Alex Hewitt's favorite mark. He was a genuine Bay Harbor bad boy. And the dictionary definition of the perfect idiot.

The first time Alex Hewitt saw me, his mouth opened wide, and his eyes got all big and excited. Guy in a wheelchair! The concept was a real whopper for him. And then he realized I wasn't from Maine, or even American—that I came from England and my mum talked weird. I was a bully's ultimate unicorn, and his brain started hatching all sorts of evil plans to make my life miserable whenever my mother wasn't around.

Alex had succeeded in making my life miserable plenty of times. At school, outside school, wherever he and his friends managed to corner me. He seemed to spend his life waiting for me to show up. Mum knew it. She went to see his father lots of times when I came home with my face bruised or my clothes torn. Or that time I got stuck on the beach because Alex and his friends pushed me into the sand and ran away with my chair to see if I could escape the tide all by myself. I'd been told that Alex's father gave him hell every time my mother went to his house to complain. Alex must have thought that torturing me was worth the trouble.

• • •

I was trying not to think about him, hoping he and his friends were busy elsewhere, torturing something else weaker than them. I was going fast to catch up with the girls, and running all sorts of scenarios in my head. I would say hello. They would say hello back. Then we would be friends for life. I had a funny feeling, like I didn't want them to see me and realize that I was special needs. But I *did* want them to see me for a bunch of other reasons.

"Oh, crap," I said when I saw Alex and his friends sitting on a bench by the town square, smoking cigarettes. I kept heading straight for the pier, which was a bold move. I knew exactly what they would do if they saw me. Trapping me on the pier was a Sunday Super Jackpot for bullies. I mumbled some choice words under my breath and reached the pier at medium to high speed.

The Goolz girls were sitting right at the end, hanging their legs over the edge, and looking down into the water. I glanced over my shoulder. Alex and his gang were heading my way, and I was pretty sure they weren't coming to take a good look at the water. I shivered. I never dared to go onto the pier without my mother when those goons were around. I wasn't sure how far they were willing to go. Would they really throw me in the freezing water? Would they even hesitate? Would they care if I drowned?

And then the girls stood and walked off in the other direction. I was risking my life to meet them, and they didn't even notice me. But by then, I had too much momentum, and there was nowhere else to go, so soon the boards of the pier were beating a fast rhythm under my wheels. I must have looked like I wanted to roll right off the edge and fly away.

But just before the edge, I came to a stop and waited. There was no way I was getting away from them now. Alex and his friends deliberately made a ton of noise catching up with me. They even howled. It was a total lose-lose situation. I'd lost the Goolz girls and gotten a pack of bullies instead.

I spun around and set the brakes on my chair. I was trapped. They were in a line all the way across the pier, with Alex in the center. He wasn't even the tallest or the biggest in their gang. He was small and thin and dressed in worn-out clothes and beaten-up shoes. It was his limitless cruelty that made him the boss.

"You waiting for the ferry, English boy?" he shouted. "It doesn't run on weekends."

"I came for the view."

That made them laugh for some reason. There were five of them, Alex's entire army of thugs.

"He's not here for the ferry. He wants to go for a swim," Peter said. "Right?"

Peter, also known as Pit Bull, was second in command. Unlike Alex, he was massive, his body already as big as an adult's. He was the muscle, the one to hold the victims down while Alex punched them and the others watched and laughed. If Alex pushed me off my wheelchair on the beach, Pit Bull would be the one to throw it out of my reach.

"A swim?" Alex nodded, his eyes boring into me. "Brilliant."

He leaned down and pressed his hands on the arms of my chair, pushing it back a little. He always went for the chair. Even after a couple years of seeing me in it, he still seemed to think I used it just to annoy him.

"Want to see the water real close, English boy?"

"Dude! There's people watching," Ronny said worriedly. He was the weak link in their gang. He was even smaller and thinner than Alex and most of the time just stood by, clearly wishing he were somewhere else.

"That's good, Ronny-boy," Alex said. "They're going to enjoy the show."

Alex's face was practically touching mine. He was getting so excited, I'm sure his mouth was watering. He turned to his friends. "You think he's gonna float?"

"I can't swim." I hated how my voice sounded, like I was pleading when I should have told him to go to hell. "If you push me off, I'll drown."

"You won't drown. You'll float, English boy."

He twisted the chair around and pushed me toward the edge. I grabbed at the wheels helplessly. They weren't turning, but the chair kept sliding toward the fall. "Stop!" I yelled.

But that got him even more excited. He gave my

chair little pushes, bringing me closer and closer to the edge.

"Hop! Hop! Hop!" he said, tilting my chair toward the water while his friends cheered and laughed.

"Push him!" Peter said. "He can't walk, but he can fly."

I clung to the rims as tightly as I could as I started sliding off the seat. Thirty feet below, angry waves hit the pier with foamy, brown, icy water. They would swallow me in seconds. I didn't want to cry. I didn't want to give them the satisfaction. But I tried too hard. A tear ran down my face and dropped into the waves.

"You stop that right now," someone said, loud and clear.

• • •

There are many ways to meet someone. When I met Ilona Goolz, I was in quite a pickle. The second Alex righted my chair and let go, I released the brakes, grabbed the wheels, and moved away from the edge, my heart thumping painfully against my chest. She was standing in front of the boys, her little sister by her side.

"Are you all right?" she asked me.

I immediately liked her voice, even before I learned to love it. I nodded. I didn't want to speak. I was scared my own voice would come out all weak and shaky.

"You witless, fart-grade idiots!" her little sister said to the boys. She pointed a finger at Alex and spoke a couple foreign, guttural words that sounded like a gypsy curse.

"What'd she say to me?" Alex asked, taking a step away from her.

"She said you're a moron," Ilona translated for him. "That goes for your friends, too."

"We're no morons." Alex looked around at his friends and spat on the pier, trying to look manly. "We were just having fun. It's not like we were really going to throw him in the water. We just wanted to scare him a little."

He was getting uneasy. She was staring at him, her long black hair hiding half her face. I took in her black dress, her coat, her huge blue eyes, the certainty in her voice, the tension in her body. I'd never seen such a beautiful creature. And I was absolutely sure Alex had never seen a girl like her either.

"That's the difference between you and me," she said, starting to walk toward him. "I'd have no problem pushing *you* over the edge."

His face became a huge question mark as she powered forward. A wave of panic went through the other guys and they scrambled out of her way. Even giant Peter did an awkward one-two-step sideways. It was way too late when Alex realized she wasn't bluffing.

He shouted, "No!" and screamed as she bulldozed him right over the edge. His scream went on for a surreally long time. It was a serious fall from the pier to the water. Then we heard him splash hard into the waves.

Ilona's little sister went all the way to the end to look down. "He's not floating," she said flatly.

I didn't want to go and see. I never wanted to be close to that edge again. Alex's friends didn't move either. They didn't charge at Ilona. Or yell at her. I guess even bullies recognize danger when they see it.

She finally nodded, giving them permission to move, and they ran past her to kneel at the edge. "Keep swimming!" Peter shouted, his voice high-pitched with panic.

The two girls came up to me. They looked pretty calm for people who had just done the unbelievable.

"I'm Ilona Goolz," Ilona said over the gurgling echoes of Alex's screams. We shook hands. "I believe I'm your new neighbor."

3

A PLUM
TOO
HIGH

When I was seven and we had just immigrated to the States from England, I stepped up on an old garden chair to reach for a plum on a high branch. I was just about to grab it when, *poof*, the chair collapsed under my feet and broke into a thousand pieces. I flew backward and cracked my back on a rock. When I opened my eyes, I was lying on the grass, looking up at blue sky through branches. I didn't call for help. I didn't yell. I just stayed there, half my body completely numb, until Mum found me. "You don't need to cry," I told her. "It was a really old chair."

"I don't remember saying that about the chair. Mum told me," I said to the Goolz as we walked home. "Just like she told me that she went running down the street, calling for help and carrying me in her arms."

It felt good telling them why I used a wheelchair. I never talked about it, and people almost never asked. But Suzie, the younger sister, asked me right away.

"It's silly," I said. "I never even liked plums that much anyway."

"It wasn't your fault," Suzie said. "It was just a plum too high."

The Goolz girls couldn't have been more different. Ilona's long black hair and tall, thin, almost ethereal body made Suzie's curly blondness and boyish features seem that much more earthly. Unlike her sister, Suzie didn't look like the dress-wearing type. She was more into jeans, mismatched socks, and old, shapeless sweaters—perfect outfits for rolling in the mud or building a tree house.

"What was that thing you said to them on the pier?" I asked her as she squatted to observe a snail on the side of the road. "It wasn't English. It sounded like you were casting a spell."

"Oh, that." She picked up the snail. "That wasn't a spell. It was Turkish for 'you dumb cucumber.' It's a common curse there."

"Dumb cucumber. That's a good one," I said, laughing. "You guys speak Turkish?"

"Yep," Suzie said and ran toward home, taking the snail along for the ride.

"We spent a year in Istanbul. We move a lot," Ilona explained. "Would you like to come over for tea?"

I didn't like tea any more than I liked plums, but I said, "I'd love to."

We reached their house and I struggled to roll across the sand, doing my best to look like I was totally acing it. I stopped at the front stairs, which was as far as I could go by myself.

"Do you want us to help you?" Ilona asked.

"If you want," I said, as though there were another option. I showed them the best way to manage stairs, and they carefully pulled me up backward. As soon as we went over the last step, I grabbed the wheels and twisted around, then followed them through the door.

Suzie dropped her coat on the floor. "Don't mind anything Dad says. He's way cuckoo."

Ilona picked up Suzie's coat and took my jacket, which wasn't such a good idea since their house was freezing. She dropped all our coats on a pile of boxes in the hall and looked up the staircase. She breathed out fog, proving it really was abnormally cold, and shook

26

her head. "Oh, no," she said. "I'm not sure you should be here right now."

Suzie shrugged. "This is going to be interesting," she said. "Do you want cocoa instead of tea? I'm going to make cocoa for everybody."

I looked upstairs with Ilona. "What's up there?"

"Dad. Doing his thing," she said flatly.

She had no idea how amazing it was for me to imagine Frank Goolz up there "doing his thing."

"Come on then," Ilona said. I followed her to the kitchen. There were piles of unopened wooden crates everywhere. Suzie dug through a carton on the kitchen counter and pulled out two cups and a bowl. Mum's cheesecake sat on the kitchen table, a single slice missing.

"Want some cake?" Ilona asked and a drawer opened all by itself right behind her. She looked down at it, took out a huge knife, and bumped the drawer closed with her hip. She smiled at me like everything was normal.

"Old house," she said, and a cupboard opened in the same spooky fashion, nearly hitting her in the head. She sighed and closed it with the tip of the knife. I shivered, either from the cold or from the weirdness of the kitchen—probably both.

Suzie started filling a pan at the sink. "We make our

cocoa with water," she told me. "Dad's special recipe since he always forgets to buy milk. Hope you like it."

"Uh-huh. Sure." Their cocoa technique was the least of my worries.

Suzie took out a fancy metal container and began pouring cocoa powder into the bowl and cups, spilling nearly as much on the counter.

Ilona frowned at her. "Could you be more careful?"

The bowl seemed to react to that: it slid gracefully off the counter and shattered on the floor with a loud crash.

"Wasn't me!" Suzie said, as the pot on the stove made a sharp metallic noise in apparent disapproval of the bowl's suicide.

"That's it!" Ilona dropped the knife on the table by the cake. "DAD!" she yelled and stormed out of the kitchen. I could hear her running up the stairs. I stared at the knife, scared to see what it might do on its own.

Suzie started wiping cocoa powder off the counter onto the floor. "We didn't make the cake," she told me. "Someone gave it to us."

"It was my mum. She made the cake." I couldn't take my eyes off the knife.

"Your mother's nice." Suzie's hands were now

covered in cocoa powder. She decided to deal with that by licking them thoroughly.

Suddenly, I noticed that I'd stopped shivering. I tried the fog test. It wasn't cold anymore. "It's warm now," I said.

Suzie must have thought I was talking about the water. She tested it with a finger that she'd just been licking. "Not yet." She took another bowl from the box and put it on the counter beside the cups.

"Stay!" she told the bowl, pointing at it with a menacing finger. And then she laughed.

I turned around when I heard footsteps coming down the stairs. Ilona was holding her father's hand, guiding him as if he were blind. His thick hair stuck out at all angles.

"This is Harold," she said as they entered the kitchen.

"Hello." He smiled, but his eyes looked past me.

"You broke a bowl," Suzie told him, pointing at the broken glass on the floor.

He scrutinized the pieces as he sat down at the table. "Sorry, darling," he told Suzie.

"Actually, it fell while you were upstairs," I said, a little too loudly. Everyone ignored me.

He scratched the salt-and-pepper stubble on his

chin, slid his chair closer to the broken bowl, then reached down and touched the spilled cocoa. He looked at it on his fingertip like an investigator.

"Did you notice anything unusual about the way the cocoa spread on the floor?" he asked Suzie.

"Like what?"

"Like patterns appearing all by themselves. Letters. Symbols. Shapes, maybe."

"No. It tastes nice, that's all."

He sighed and slid his chair back to the table.

Suzie brought the cups and bowl to the table and poured the hot water, then found another cup and made instant coffee for her dad. She gave me the bowl. The cocoa looked particularly dark with just water and no milk. I tried it. It tasted awful.

Ilona served us all slices of cheesecake.

"You made a cake, darling?" her dad asked.

"My mother made the cake," I said. "She gave it to you like an hour ago."

"Oh. Really? That's nice," he said, looking at the cake like it was another mystery to solve.

Ilona got spoons out of the drawer that had magically opened. Only this time, she opened it the old-fashioned way. We all ate some cake. It was good. Mum is ace at baking.

After a few bites, Frank Goolz turned to me and frowned. "Who are you?"

"Dad!" Ilona said.

"I'm your neighbor. I live next door with my mum."

"Yes, of course. The cake. The neighbor. I remember now." He smiled and patted my shoulder.

But then he frowned again and leaned toward me. "Did you notice anything strange about the cocoa?" he asked.

"I . . . prefer it with milk."

"I mean the powder," he said impatiently. "Did you notice anything strange about the powder? On the floor? When the bowl broke, maybe?"

I shook my head.

He kept staring at me. "Are you absolutely sure? You're not hiding something? Out of *fear*, maybe?"

I shook my head again. I *was* feeling a little fearful, but mostly because of him.

He finally sighed and stood up from the table. "This is not working." He picked up his coffee cup and left the room, abandoning his cake half eaten.

"No more tricks!" Ilona called after him as he wandered back upstairs.

"Yeah," Suzie agreed, running after him. "No more tricks, Dad! We don't have any more bowls."

Ilona stood staring after her father and Suzie for a long moment. I wanted to ask her a ton of questions—like where their mother was. Or why they had come to live in Bay Harbor. Or the big one—what their father was doing upstairs that could break bowls downstairs.

"I don't think I made a good impression on him," I said instead. "He was very disappointed with my cocoa-observation skills."

She gave me her beautiful smile. "You were fine. He's really not always like this." She squatted to pick up the broken glass. "I mean, he's always weird, but not *that* weird. His new project is driving him nuts, or sick. Or both."

"A new book?"

"More like an experiment he shouldn't be doing with an artifact he shouldn't own."

"You mean, like a scientific experiment?" I asked.

She wet a towel in the sink and then turned and looked at me intensely, like she was making up her mind. "I'm sorry, Harold. I'm not supposed to talk about it."

"Oh, okay," I said, and my breath came out in a puff of fog.

Ilona shivered, her breath coming out in a cloud too.

"It's freezing," I said. "Is your dad . . . doing his thing again?"

My bowl twitched in my hand like an animal trying to escape. I set it down and it slid right off the table and smashed on the floor, splattering watery cocoa all over.

"Wasn't me!" I said, just like Suzie had.

"I know." Ilona dropped her towel over the new mess on the floor. "Should I help you get back to your place?"

It wasn't really a question. It was a way to tell me that she wanted me to go, and it hurt.

But as she helped me down the front stairs, she said, "I'm going to ask Dad to build a ramp for you. Since you'll be coming over a lot."

I liked the idea of that. And when I looked back at her as we struggled through the sand on the way to the bridge, she smiled down at me and I felt better about everything.

4

NIGHT
FLASHES

Mum stopped by my room late that night. She had a cup of tea in one hand and a bunch of files in the other.

"You're still up?" she asked.

She looked exhausted. It was one o'clock in the morning. She was working on an account for one of her clients, and she'd said it could take all night. Even from a distance, I could smell that she had been secretly smoking in our backyard. I could always tell, no matter how much soap and mint gum she used to hide it from me.

"You had a cigarette," I said, turning away from my computer screen. She blushed and called me a silly sausage and left me alone to return to her work.

I hadn't told her anything about what had happened to me, either at the pier or with the Goolz. I knew Mum wouldn't like any of it, bullies or poltergeists.

I had been Googling Frank Goolz again, trying to find out more about him and his daughters. Right then I was staring at a picture of an amazingly beautiful older version of Ilona. A note on the website said that her name was Nathalie and that she had been Frank Goolz's wife and had died many years ago. Nowhere did it say that they had two daughters. In fact, there wasn't any mention of Ilona or Suzie anywhere, as if Frank Goolz had been hiding their existence from the public.

I closed my laptop and looked at my hand, remembering how the bowl had twitched in it right before flying off the table. It was a memory my mind refused to believe or file, like a dream you can't quite remember after waking up.

I turned off the light, went to the window, and peered around my curtains at the Goolz house, making sure to stay well hidden. Most of the windows were dark, but lights still shone in a few. I wondered if Ilona was awake and which room was hers. I also wondered if she would go to my school. I imagined that we would go together every morning and Alex would run away screaming whenever he saw us. Somehow, in my fantasy,

35

he was still drenched and had seaweed hanging from his shoulders and head.

I picked up the book I had left on my desk earlier—*Voodooland*, a Frank Goolz novel I'd already read more than once. I opened it to a random page and read a couple sentences, using my phone to light the pages. The main character, a horror writer like Frank Goolz, was trapped in a cage in a sordid basement somewhere in Haiti and didn't know who his captor was. I thought of what Ilona had said about her father conducting weird experiments with forbidden artifacts. I tried to keep reading, but I couldn't stop thinking about the self-moving drawers and self-destructive cocoa bowls. A very odd thought had sprung up in my mind. What if Frank Goolz's books weren't made up? I let my phone go dark, thinking about all the Frank Goolz novels I had read. Zombies, vampires, dark entities from other dimensions, and lots and lots of other monsters. Were they *all* based on something real?

"That's impossible," I said out loud and looked at their house again.

The light in the window right across from mine had been switched off. I felt sure that it was Ilona's room for some reason. I heard Mum curse and call her client all sorts of names, and it made me smile. I closed the curtains and went over to my bed, wondering if I should go through the trouble of putting on my pajamas or just sleep in my clothes.

Then I came to an abrupt halt as lights started flashing into my room. It was like the paparazzi were trying to take my picture through the curtains.

"What the heck?" I went back to the window. The lights kept flashing—right into my eyes now, and I could hear loud voices outside. I pulled the curtains and squinted down at the Goolz's yard. Ilona was there, still in her black dress and coat, yelling at her father. They were both looking up at their house from a safe distance. Ilona shouted for Suzie.

The flashing light poured from most of the windows of the Goolz house, but especially the round attic window, since it didn't have blinds. Then something appeared between two flashes. "Crap on a stick!" I yelled.

Through the window, inside the Goolz's attic, someone or something was staring at me in the pulse of light and darkness. It was a woman, I thought, but her skin was way too gray and her eyes were way too white. Her long, black hair hovered above her head in a huge, tight bun—a style that belonged to a time long gone. Her blouse looked filthy and wet, as if she had just crawled out of mud, and the scarf around her neck was covered in dark goo that could have been blood, once upon a time.

"She's not real," I said to myself. She stood so still, I thought for a second she could be a mannequin or a horror movie poster glued to the window by one of the Goolz for the purpose of scaring me to death. I leaned in and looked more carefully. Her lips moved to form an evil, cadaverous grin. She touched the window with a hand that seemed to have lost most of its flesh. Just bones and rotten nails remained. She waved at me.

This was no picture.

This was a living, grinning, waving mummified monster!

"Mum!" I screamed, shoving away from the window.

"What?!" Mum ran into my room and saw the lights and our flashing shadows on the walls and me cowering by the window. "What's going on out there?" She looked outside.

"Do you see her?" I yelled.

"Who?"

"The woman in the attic!"

"What woman?"

"The one with the freaking rotten hands and crazy eyes!"

I came back to the window to show her. The woman was gone.

"Suzie!" Ilona yelled outside.

"What's going on?" Mum asked again.

I cursed and went past my mother to the hallway. In no time, I was sitting on the stair lift, holding tightly to my chair.

"Where are you going?" my mother called after me.

She followed me outside, carrying her yellow raincoat and my jacket, begging me to put it on, but I was too busy trying to get to Ilona to listen to my mother. I went to the bridge and struggled to cross it. On the other side, Mum pushed me through the soft wet sand. It was unusually cold out, electric cold, and the wind and rain kissed my skin in all the wrong ways.

Ilona saw me and frowned. "You shouldn't be here," she said. She looked particularly intense and unreal in the rapidly flashing lights. There was this determination in her eyes, exactly like when she pushed Alex off the pier. She turned back to the house.

"Oh, cheese," she said, and ran inside, her black coat flapping behind her.

"Ilona!" Frank Goolz called and ran into the house after her.

I went up to the front stairs. "Help me!" I begged Mum.

Mum was looking at the flashing lights, hypnotized like a bug near a light bulb.

"Mum! Help me up the stairs!"

"There is no way you're going in there."

I was about to protest, threaten, blackmail— whatever it took to get her to help me—when the flashing stopped and Frank Goolz came back out, carrying Suzie in his arms.

"Oh, my God. Is she all right?" Mum said, running over to them.

"She's all right," Frank Goolz said. He sat on the stairs, his daughter on his lap, and hugged her to his chest. Mum squatted in front of them and touched Suzie's forehead.

"She's just in a deep sleep," Frank Goolz said, his chin resting on the crown of Suzie's head.

Mum took her hand away, apparently satisfied with Suzie's temperature. "What was that?" she asked.

Frank Goolz looked back at the house over his shoulder. It was quiet and dark again. "Oh. That? Well . . . electrical problems."

Ilona came out of the house and sat beside him. She

closed her eyes and shook her head and looked terribly annoyed.

"This is over, Dad," she said fiercely. "Over!"

"It's over, Ilo," Frank Goolz agreed. "I promise." He put his arm over her shoulders and she leaned against him. It was like Mum and I weren't there anymore. The Goolz were alone in their private world of strange secrets and weird events.

5

SLEEPOVER

Mum told them to come to our place until someone could look into their "electrical problem." Frank Goolz said they were fine, but Ilona told him to accept Mum's invitation. She said that everybody would be better off at our place until daylight, when the electrical problem would surely be completely fixed.

Mum and Frank Goolz went up to our guest room to put Suzie to bed, leaving me and Ilona in the living room. I wanted to tell Ilona about the mummified woman in their attic, but I didn't know how to bring her up without sounding spooked and weird.

"Your mom is really nice," she said. "She's really beautiful, too."

I shrugged. I thought Ilona was the beautiful one

42

right then. She was still wearing her black coat and hugging herself like she couldn't get warm as she gazed out at the moonlit beach.

I was trying not to look outside. I was too scared that the attic woman would come grinning out of the darkness. My memory of her was getting bigger and scarier in the silence between us.

"I saw something in your house," I blurted. "I saw something really strange."

She turned to me, suddenly looking awfully serious. "What did you see?"

"A woman. In your attic. She grinned at me."

Shrub branches knocked against the glass in a gust of wind and I jumped.

"It's just the wind," Ilona said. She came to sit beside me. "What did she look like?" I realized she was taking me seriously.

"She looked horrible. Her eyes. Her skin. Her hands!" I made my hands into claws to show her, then shook my head. "I can't even describe it and not sound crazy. Are you . . . are you hiding a dead lady in your attic?"

It sounded ridiculous, but she didn't laugh.

"There's only the three of us," she replied.

"Who is she, then?"

She thought for a while, looking at me with an intensity that told me she really did believe me.

"Do you know who she is?" I asked again.

"I think I do."

"Who, then?"

She stared at me silently, then put her hand on mine. It felt great, even though we were talking about a grinning cadaver popping up in their window in the middle of the night.

"She's someone who should have been left undisturbed," she said finally.

Her answer triggered a serious chill all the way down my back, plus another million questions, but Mum and Frank Goolz came down the stairs and Ilona took her hand away.

"Don't say anything. It would drive Dad nuts," she whispered.

"Let's get you guys to bed," Mum said. "Thank God it's not a school night." She took a better look at me. "Are you all right?"

I must have looked like a fish that had come face-to-face with a shark.

"I'm fine," I said, and took a quick look at Ilona.

She nodded and muttered, "Thank you," which felt great, too.

"Ilona can have my room. I'll sleep down here," I said. I didn't want her to see me sitting on the stair lift.

Mum handed out clean towels and gave one of my Universal Classic Monsters T-shirts to Ilona to use as pajamas. Mum was excellent at creating order out of chaos. She'd been doing exactly that since the day I fell out of the plum tree.

"Good night," Ilona said, holding my T-shirt tight against her as she climbed the stairs with her father. I did a silly military salute that I thought would look cool. And it might have worked, since it made her smile.

"She's a very nice girl," Mum said once the Goolz had disappeared upstairs. She turned her gaze on me. "And she's very pretty."

I shrugged, trying to look like I hadn't noticed. Mum opened the sofa bed and I transferred my body onto it.

She sat beside me. "I'm going to sleep down here with you."

"If you want," I said, but secretly I was relieved. I turned my back to the glass doors, my eyes wide open.

Mum covered me with a blanket and said she would phone her handyman tomorrow and ask him to look into the Goolz's electrical problem. She said Frank Goolz was a very interesting man—though, she

45

confirmed, he really was as weird as a blue carrot. She said it was funny that they ended up sleeping at our place on the very first night they arrived in Bay Harbor.

"Mum," I said finally. "Let's go to sleep."

"Oh. Yes. Sure, pumpkin." She kissed me on the shoulder and stretched out beside me. I had my back to her, but I knew that her eyes were wide open, too. I was pretty sure she kept babbling silently inside her head, probably secretly happy that the Goolz had electrical problems. I knew she was imagining all sorts of scenarios where we became inseparable best friends with the Goolz, because I was running the exact same scenarios in my own head.

But my scenarios were peppered with the flashing image of the lady in the attic, grinning her dead grin.

. . .

I woke up with a weird feeling. Mum was snoring gently beside me. She had turned off all the lights while I was sleeping. Cinders were still glowing in the fireplace, projecting warm red shadows on the white walls. It smelled of burning wood and comfort. It took me a while to find the nerve to rise onto my elbow and look over my shoulder at the veranda. It was nearly dawn and the sky over the ocean was slowly lightening, erasing last night's nightmare. I heard the sisters talking upstairs and pushed Mum over so I could get off the sofa.

"Gotta save those rabbits," she said in her sleep, and started snoring again.

The lift made a deafening mechanical noise, squealing through the silence of the house. I could see Mum twisting and turning on the sofa, fighting hard not to let the noise fully wake her. She finally grabbed a pillow and put it over her head, still muttering about rabbits. I thought the girls must have heard me coming, too. The lift was noisy enough to wake the dead, especially when it reached the top. By the time I got back in my chair, they'd dropped their voices to whispers.

Ilona had left the door to my room wide open. The wooden floorboards creaked under my weight and the whispering stopped altogether. I approached at extra-slow speed with the feeling that I was disturbing something.

"Oh, hello," I said.

Ilona was sitting up in bed, her back against the wall, dressed in my absolute favorite T-shirt: Frankenstein's monster holding his bride's hand. Suzie was sitting beside her, wearing my long-sleeved Creature from the Black Lagoon shirt.

"Ilona said you saw her," Suzie barked at me.

Ilona hushed her. "You're going to wake everybody," she said.

I went into my room and shut the door.

"Did you, then?" Suzie whispered.

"I saw something. Or someone. I don't know."

"What do you mean, you don't know?" she snapped. "You saw her, right?"

"Stop shouting," Ilona said.

Suzie switched back to whispering. "It was my mom you saw."

"Isn't your mum . . ."

"She's dead all right," she said. "But she's coming back for us."

I turned to Ilona.

"It wasn't our mother," she said, more to Suzie than to me. "It was nobody. A trick of the mind. An illusion."

"Why would you say that?" Suzie gave her a nasty push and pointed at me. "He saw her. He's paralyzed, not blind."

"Suzie, that's enough," Ilona said, grabbing her by the arm.

We looked at each other silently for a while. My room was getting bright fast. The heavy curtains could never stop the tsunami of sunlight coming over the ocean first thing in the morning.

"I'm sorry," Suzie said to me and Ilona let go of her arm. "I didn't mean to hurt your feelings."

"It's all right. You didn't," I lied.

She stood up and walked past me to the door, then stopped. "What was she like?" she asked. "I mean, what did she look like? Was she pretty?"

"I don't know," I said. "It was very fast. I'm not even sure I saw her for real. Maybe it was just an illusion, like Ilona said."

I was lying about that, too. I knew I saw her and I knew she was real. And she wasn't anywhere close to pretty.

"My mother was really pretty," Suzie snapped, like I was silly for not having noticed. She walked into the hallway, muttering something in a foreign language, probably calling me all sorts of cucumbers.

We heard the boards creak under her feet all the way to the guest room.

"I shouldn't have told her," Ilona said. "Now she's going to tell Dad, and they're both going to go nuts about it."

I nodded and moved closer to her. It felt oddly

49

familiar seeing her in my room, sitting on my bed, wearing my T-shirt.

"It's Dad's fault. He puts all those crazy ideas in her head. He doesn't realize how much it affects her."

The sun kept pouring in, projecting the deep blue color of the curtains all over the walls.

"I like your room," she said, looking around. "I haven't had a real room in forever. I mean, a room filled with my own things instead of just a mattress on the floor and a bunch of boxes."

I looked around my room, rediscovering it through her eyes. I had plenty of my own things. All my books and comics were piled on my desk and shelves. An old space-age black-and-white TV from the 70s stood in the corner. It even sort of worked if you punched it on the left side the right way. On top of the TV, my collection of DC comics and Marvel figurines faced each other, a Star Wars stormtrooper clock standing guard between them. A ray of sunshine hit my vintage poster of the Hulk, lighting up his snarling face.

Suzie came running back from the guest room, making enough noise to wake up the entire house. "Dad's really sick!" she yelled.

She grabbed Ilona by the sleeve and pulled her out of bed, knocking the blanket to the floor. I had to lean

50

down and move it out of the way to follow them.

"What's going on? Why aren't you guys sleeping?" Mum asked when I came into the hall. Her hair was all messed up, and her bathrobe was loosely tied and twisted all around her.

"Something about their dad," I said, and we followed Ilona and Suzie into the guest room.

"I'm all right," Frank Goolz said as we entered.

He didn't look all right at all. Mum had found a shirt for him to change into, but he was so drenched in sweat, it looked like someone had thrown a bucket of water at him. His eyes were wandering and unfocused, and he could hardly lift himself up on his arms.

Mum sat on the edge of the bed and touched his forehead with the back of her hand. "You're burning up."

"Yes, that's quite normal," he said.

Mum stood up and readjusted her bathrobe. "I'm driving you to the emergency room."

"No, you're not," he said, pulling on Ilona's arm to help him sit up. "I need to get back to my house. Fast. Ilona?"

She nodded and helped him stand. He wobbled on his legs, leaning against her.

"He'll be all right," she said.

I backed up, and Mum moved out of their way.

Suzie picked up her dad's shoes and came to help Ilona support him. Mum and I looked at each other. I shrugged and she shook her head.

"Mr. Goolz," she said. "Frank. You look extremely ill."

"I'll be fine," he said, wobbling toward the stairs between his daughters.

"Ilona, I don't think your father is in a good state to decide what's right for him," Mum said.

We followed them to the stairs.

"He never really is," Ilona answered. "I'll come by later to pick up our things."

We watched them go down the stairs and walk to the front door.

"Bye-bye, then," Frank Goolz mumbled. He made a failed attempt at waving.

"Thank you for having us," Ilona said, struggling to open the door.

"What about your electrical problem?" Mum asked.

"It's fixed," Ilona said. She slammed the door behind them.

Mum and I stayed at the top of the stairs, staring at our front door for a while.

"Strange people," Mum said. "Right?"

I thought about what Suzie had said about her mother and remembered the vision of the dead lady in the attic. I thought of Ilona, too. Mostly I thought of Ilona, sitting on my bed, wearing my Bride of Frankenstein T-shirt and admiring my Hulk poster.

"Interesting people," I said. We went down to start breakfast.

6

BACK TO SCHOOL,
AND
NOT

Monday came and with it the obligation to go back to school and face Alex Hewitt. I hooked my schoolbag on the back of my chair with a sense of impending doom. The only thing that got me going was the fantasy that the Goolz girls would join me on the way to school.

And that day, my fantasy came true. Ilona was sitting on her porch, a backpack by her side. She stood up when she saw me.

"I was starting to think you'd already left," she said. My heart made a full revolution inside my chest. "Or that you were homeschooled and I'd have to go all by myself."

"I thought you might be in high school," I said.

"You'd have to take the bus to Newton High. It's, like, light-years away."

"I'm in seventh grade."

"Me too," I said. "We'll be in the same class. Alex is in our class, too. He's fourteen, but he defies the laws of nature when it comes to learning things."

"Who's Alex?"

"The guy you pushed off the pier."

"Oh. That guy. Consider him neutralized."

I didn't think Alex's kind of evil could ever be neutralized, but I liked that she said it.

"Where's Suzie?" I asked.

"She's staying home with Dad, pretending she's sick, too. That's what she always does to get out of going to school."

"How's your dad?" I asked.

"Much better. You should tell your mother. I saw her staring at our house, looking seriously worried."

We went along silently for a while. I wanted to ask her about Suzie and why she thought the monster I saw was their mother. In fact, I still had a million questions about the lady in the attic. I didn't know how to ask any of them.

"So your sister's not really sick?" I asked finally.

"Nah. She just hates school. And she likes to stay

with Dad all the time. They're really close. They both belong in the nuthouse." Somehow it didn't sound like a bad thing when she said it. "I'm sure she's going to become a weirdo writer, just like him."

"You don't want to be a writer?"

"No way." She tapped her forehead. "I'm not crazy enough to be a writer."

"What do you want to be, then?"

She shrugged. "Dunno. Something that lets me travel all the time. Like some kind of explorer maybe."

Her words made me smile. Traveling and exploring were at the top of my list too.

"And you?" she asked.

"Me?"

"What's your big plan for the future?"

"Oh." I looked at her and smiled. "The NBA, obviously."

She laughed. I loved making her laugh.

. . .

Ilona sat beside me in homeroom. I turned around to look at Alex in his usual seat, way at the back. His arms were tightly crossed, and he was doing a good job of pretending that Ilona and I were invisible, which was a dramatic change from his usual habit of running his finger across his neck whenever he caught me looking at him.

When we left the classroom, Alex lingered in the back, leaning against the wall. For once, he didn't rush to the door to give my chair a good kick on his way out. And once he got to the hall, he rejoined his pack of goons, and they went the other way, probably to find a sixth-grader to stuff in a locker. I looked up at Ilona. She smiled back. Maybe she really had gotten Alex and his gang off my back for good.

We went to our lockers, which were right across the hall from each other.

"*Kismet*," she said.

"What?"

"*Kismet*," she repeated. "You know, the Turkish word for 'destiny'?"

I didn't know, but I was happy that she saw the locations of our lockers as the work of destiny. I took out my English book, then crossed the hall to her locker. It had been cleaned recently. You could see the marks of stickers that had been scraped off.

"B hearts G," she said, reading what was scratched into the metal. "That's funny. Your last name is Bell, right? Bell hearts Goolz. That works."

"That is funny," I said, feeling blood rushing to my cheeks.

"I don't believe in love," she said. "People look so stupid when they're in love. Don't you think?"

I came crashing down from my high. "Yeah, totally."

"I don't want my mind to go all mushy with useless feelings. I want to see people for what they really are." She looked at me very intently. "I don't know you very well, but I like who you are, Harold Bell."

"I like who you are too, Ilona Goolz," I said.

"Oh, cheese, Harold, you don't need to blush about it," she said, but I thought she might be blushing a little too.

She unfolded the class schedule. "English's next. Mrs. Richer. Interesting?"

"Oh, deadly."

. . .

Mrs. Richer was as exciting as a dead slug drying under the sun. She also had the superpower of making every second last twice as long. Ilona was sharing my English book and we were writing notes like "Bored," "Dying here," "I think time just stopped," and "One of my back molars just fell off. Help!"

I laughed aloud at that one and Mrs. Richer looked up at us.

"Sorry," I said.

Then Ilona wrote, "Look out the window."

I did and saw a pair of big, blue eyes staring at us from the other side. Suzie stuck her lips against the glass and blew up her cheeks. Half the class started laughing, but Suzie had disappeared by the time Mrs. Richer looked. Ilona wrote another note on the English book: "Wish we were out there with her." The bell rang, freeing us from this slow-cooking torture.

"She makes reading Poe feel like a kick in the head," Ilona said, shoving books in her bag. "And I love Poe."

Mrs. Richer must have heard her. She gave us a dirty look as we left the classroom.

Suzie was waiting for us in the hall, casually leaning against the wall.

"You're supposed to be at home with Dad," Ilona said.

"Dad's sleeping. I was bored."

"There's always school," I suggested.

"That's even more boring." She followed us to our lockers. I opened mine to drop off my English book and get my stuff for math, but the girls didn't stop with me—they were heading straight for the exit. I left my math book in my locker and closed the padlock in a hurry to catch up with them.

"Where are you going?" I asked. "Our first break isn't for another hour. We have only five minutes to get to Mr. Chalmer's class."

"Is the famous Mr. Chalmer as charismatic as Mrs. Richer?" Ilona asked.

I thought for a minute. "About the same, but louder, and with really bad breath."

"Exactly my point," Ilona said. They kept walking toward the door.

I stopped for a second, watching them. "We can't do this," I said, but I knew perfectly well that we were.

"Come enjoy the world!" Suzie called back at me.

Skipping school sounded like a bad idea. But enjoying the world instead of being trapped in a classroom sounded like a freaking great one.

"We're going to get so busted for this," I said, but I was so excited I couldn't have cared less.

Ilona leaned on the door, and it opened, letting in a blast of sunshine. "My dear Harold. There's no true adventure without a high sense of danger and the possibility of peril."

"Amen to that," I said and followed them out.

7

THE
OWL
HOUSE

We soon realized we weren't the only ones too cool for school. We saw Alex Hewitt coming around the side of the building, and Suzie immediately decided we should spy on him. She started running after him before I could try to talk her out of it. We hurried to catch up.

"There's no stopping her, is there?" I asked Ilona.

"Nope."

We followed Alex all the way to the edge of Bay Harbor and well onto the road to Newton. He refused to go in a straight line and zigzagged everywhere, taking the time to kick or destroy whatever looked breakable along the way.

Alex was now walking down a stretch of dead grass toward the line of trees that hid the Hewitt farm. "He's going home," I realized.

People almost never dared to go near the Hewitt grounds, especially on foot. The Hewitts had a large pack of dogs that barked constantly, and Alex's father was known for loving liquor and violence. He was a nasty giant with graying red hair and a huge beard eating up his face. He mostly stayed on his own secluded property, but sometimes he came into town to go to Gilmore's Tavern with his friend Donahue. When that happened everyone knew to stay away and try not to upset them.

"If Old Hewitt takes a disliking to you, he'll let you know the hard way," I said as we passed the old abandoned church. "That's what people say around here. They're all scared of him."

"What about Alex's mother? An ogress?"

"Mum heard that she ran away years ago, leaving Alex behind. People say she was horrible too."

"They sound like a real family of trolls," Ilona said, but she didn't sound concerned.

"Listen!" I said, grabbing Ilona's wrist. The Hewitts' dogs barked raucously in the distance. We had gone way past the wall at the edge of the old cemetery, which was already far into the Hewitt no-go zone.

"What're we waiting for?" Suzie asked, looking back at us.

I watched Alex disappear behind the thick line of trees. The dogs barked louder.

"Look over there." I pointed at two moving black dots at the edge of the trees. "Dogs! We need to go before they spot us and decide we're their next meal."

Thankfully, Ilona agreed. We started retracing our steps back toward the abandoned church. Suzie kept glancing back at the Hewitt grounds, disappointed that our mission had been called off. She picked up a stick and was about to throw it in the general direction of the dogs. But then she turned her attention to the church and whistled admiringly.

"It was abandoned a long time ago," I said, as though I knew everything about it. I knew nothing about it.

"Do you hear that?" Ilona asked, moving closer to the church.

The dogs were quieter now. Suzie put her ear to the old white board of the wall. "There's something moving inside."

"Rats?" I suggested.

"Rats or something better," Suzie said. We followed her as she walked around the building, looking for a way in. She reached the front door and inspected the rusted padlock and chain.

"I've always wondered what it looks like inside," I said.

"Let's find out," Suzie said. She put her stick through the padlock and started yanking.

"We're really going to break in?" I asked, turning to Ilona.

She shrugged. "I guess we are," she said. "I'm kind of curious too."

I tried to play it cool, as though breaking and entering was nothing special.

The stick broke and Suzie cursed in a foreign language—German, I thought. She took a few steps away and contemplated the building, then picked up what was left of her stick and walked around the church, smacking the rotting white boards as she searched for another solution.

"She's stubborn, just like Dad," Ilona said, sitting on the grass beside my chair. "They bite into something and never let go."

Suzie got down on her knees and scratched the earth at the base of the building.

"Did you guys talk more about the other night?" I asked. "About the lights. And the . . ." I didn't know how to put it.

"The scary lady in the attic," Ilona finished for me. "Suzie still believes you saw the ghost of our mother. She doesn't get that it was just an illusion."

I nodded, but secretly I agreed with Suzie. I wanted to believe Ilona more than anything, but I knew for sure that it hadn't been an illusion. The high-definition image of the grinning cadaver and her empty, dead eyes kept popping up in my mind. I wanted to erase it. Treat it as a trick of the mind so I could stop feeling that pinch of fear on the back of my neck each time I looked at their house from my window, which I'd done about a gazillion times since I'd seen her.

Suzie had removed enough ground to grab hold of the board at the base of the building. She broke off a large chunk of rotten wood and started scooting under on her belly.

"She's going to get stuck under there," I said.

"Oh, cheese!" Ilona said. She darted after Suzie and caught her foot right before she disappeared all the way under the church.

"Let go of me!" Suzie yelled. She kicked her sister's hand away and snaked under the building faster than a fox smelling a rabbit.

Ilona turned to me and shrugged. "She'll come out eventually. And if she doesn't, we'll have a funny story to tell Dad later."

Suzie suddenly started banging and scratching hard. I went closer to the building. The noise abruptly stopped.

"Oh. Spiders," she said calmly. And then there was a loud *bang* and a huge CRACK.

"Are you all right?" I called.

"Suzie! Sign of life, please," Ilona requested.

There was no reply.

"She's impossible." Ilona banged her fist on the wall. "Suzie!"

"What?" Suzie said. She came around the corner of the building, covered in spiderwebs, dust, and dirt, a victorious smile on her face. "You guys have *got* to see this."

We followed her around the building. Ilona was right about her sister. Once she had an idea in her mind, nothing could stop her.

Suzie had unlocked the back door from inside. A toxic cloud of stink hit us as we got close.

"Wow," I said, covering my nose with my arm.

"Charming." Ilona did the same with her arm. "Smells like a broken toilet in there."

They helped me into the building. The stink inside

was unbearable. It was so strong it made my eyes sting. The benches, the floor, the pulpit, everything was covered in a thick white and gray layer of bird poop. There were feathers everywhere. And there, right in the middle of the aisle, was the huge hole Suzie had dug to get into the building.

"I think owls are living here," Ilona said. She probed one of the many strange balls on the floor with the tip of her shoe. It crumbled under the pressure, displaying a mixture of fur and bones. I immediately looked up, searching for the owls.

"Owls are nice," Suzie said. "This could be our special place. You know, to come hide, plot, maybe have a picnic."

Ilona and I looked at each other.

"I'm not sure this is the right place for picnics," Ilona said.

Suzie didn't seem affected by the smell. She walked to the altar and looked up. "They're up there in their nest. There's two of them."

We went to take a look. There was a large mountain of poop and many more fur balls at the edge of the pulpit. And directly above, on the corner of a large beam, I saw the nest and two huge white-and-gray masses inside it.

One of them moved. It turned its face, opened its huge eyes, and looked straight at me. It was an actual freaking owl.

"This is amazing," I said, my eyes wide. "I've never seen an owl before. IRL."

I smiled and turned to Ilona. She was still looking up, mesmerized just like me. I never would have imagined that these mysterious great birds were hiding in this rotting old building. I had to wait for the Goolz to come into my life for a chance to see them with my own eyes.

"Have you guys ever seen an owl before?" I asked.

"Of course," Suzie said. She was trying to sound blasé, but I could tell she was as excited as me.

"Hello, owls!" she called. "We're going to share your home from now on."

She turned to her sister. "I'm going to bring them mice. Do you know where I can buy mice? Maybe I can catch some. Owls love mice."

One of the owls tilted its head as though pleased by the idea of home-delivered mice. But then dogs started barking and we quickly forgot about mice, owls, and even the bird poop. We all turned to the wide-open door. Suzie ran to close and lock it.

We heard the dogs start scratching the walls, panting and yapping along the way.

And then I heard Alex Hewitt's voice. "Easy now. Woop! Woop! Come here, boys! Don't scare them away."

Ilona approached one of the windows. It was boarded, but you could see outside through the cracks. I moved to her side as silently as I could and lifted myself off the chair a little to get a look outside. Alex was sitting on the ground, exactly where Ilona had been sitting earlier. He had a BB gun by his side and was cuddling with the dogs. I counted them—one, two, three, four. Crap! Ilona looked down at me. I shook my head. Alex, a gun, and a large pack of dogs were a terrible combination.

The dogs started running around the building and back to Alex, licking his face, rubbing against him, snuggling up to him. It was like those four black monsters were his best friends. He put the gun down and took a can of something from his jacket pocket. He pulled a huge knife out from his belt and opened the can with it, then took out a slice of something juicy and slurped it down. He threw a slice at each dog and smiled as they ran after them.

"What kind of stupid dogs like peaches, huh?" But he didn't sound like the usual Alex. He didn't look like he wanted to hurt something. He looked peaceful, taking a walk with his dogs, having a picnic on the cemetery grounds with them. Eating peaches.

He finished the can, slicing the last peaches so the dogs would get a bite each, and gulping down the juice. "Hey!" he yelled at the building. "I've got a surprise for you."

My heart started beating crazy fast. I moved away from the window, but Ilona and Suzie kept looking. After a while, there was a knock on the roof right above me.

"I got you some really fat ones," Alex yelled. Ilona turned and motioned for me to come back. Alex wasn't shouting at us. He was taking little gray balls out of his pocket and throwing them onto the roof. The dogs were getting hysterical, scratching at the walls, trying to climb up the side of the building.

"You're welcome, you ungrateful turds!" Alex yelled. Then he called his dogs, picked up his gun, and walked away, throwing the empty can into the road.

We waited a long time, listening to the barking dogs making their way back down to the Hewitt grounds. When it felt safe, we stepped out of the church. I was dizzy from fear and the smell of bird poop. The fresh air felt magical. We backed up until we could see the roof of the church. There were, like, half a dozen gray bodies up there.

"They're dead mice," Suzie said.

I shook my head. This wasn't at all the Alex Hewitt I knew. He had no intention of killing the owls or harming them in any way.

Alex Hewitt was feeding them.

8

THE
STONE OF THE
DEAD

When we tried to go back to school for afternoon classes, Mum and Ms. Hamper, the school principal, were waiting on the front steps, making faces like they were trying to swallow bugs.

"I phoned your father, too," Ms. Hamper told Ilona and Suzie. "He's not answering."

"He's sleeping," Suzie said testily. "He's been sick, and he doesn't like phone calls. Can we go now?"

Ms. Hamper sent me home for the rest of the day and said she'd keep Ilona and Suzie until their father came to claim them.

Mum walked silently beside me. She didn't seem to know how to handle the situation. This was the first time I'd skipped school. There was no doubt that

I was stubborn. I was irritable. I was a pain sometimes. But I was a good kid, a predictable kid, a kid who would never skip school. Until I met Ilona and the rest of the Goolz clan.

It took her half the way home to find the right words. "I'm . . . disappointed," she said. But she sounded more puzzled than disappointed.

"I understand you're excited to have interesting new friends. But we don't skip class. We just don't do it."

"Class was boring," I said, knowing perfectly well that she wouldn't see this as a good excuse.

She stopped walking. I pretended not to notice and kept going.

"Things are boring sometimes," she called after me. "That's how life works, Harold."

I still didn't stop.

"You plough through the ordinary parts between more exciting moments."

I finally stopped and turned to face her. "What if you reject the boring parts, and keep searching for the exciting ones? That's what the Goolz seem to do, and it works just fine for them."

"We're not the Goolz, Harold. We're normal people," she said, catching up with me. "I work. You go to school. We're doing well. As well as anyone else, even if we don't have the Goolz's exotic life."

I turned away toward the beach.

"Are you going to punish me?" I asked.

"Oh, heck yeah!" She gave me a tap on the back of the head. "Pumpkin, I'm going to get very creative on that one."

. . .

She took away my laptop, phone, and my tablet, which was painful because I'd just read *Voodooland* again and I was itching to look up stuff about Voodoo online. I had just decided to go to Mum and beg for my computer back when a tap on my window startled me. I went over to pull the curtains back just enough to peek outside. The attic window was empty—no flashing lights and no scary lady. A second tap made me look down.

"Ilona," I said, a jolt of joy zapping through me. She stood below with a handful of pebbles, waiting. I opened my window.

"Can I come up?" she asked.

"Sure, why not?" I said, trying to play it cool.

She stepped onto one of the barrels Mum used to collect rainwater and aced the climb.

"You don't need to come through the window. Mum took away my computer and phone till the end of time, but she didn't ban you from the house."

But Ilona had already reached the window, a big, wide smile on her face. "We needed to try it, for when she does."

I gave up playing Cool Harold and mirrored her big, wide smile.

She jumped in and brushed off her hands on her black coat. "Now we know it works. There's no way your mother can keep us apart."

I knew she was joking, but it made my smile a notch wider anyway.

"Harold?" Mum called from her office. "Who are you talking to?"

"Ilona's here!" I shouted.

A long silence followed. Mum probably regretted not establishing a complete Goolz embargo.

"You kids be good! And I mean *really* good. No funny business!"

"Mum!"

Ilona shouted back, "No funny business!" She winked and stuck her tongue out at me. Funny business was definitely on the menu.

She plopped down on my bed and took off her coat. "This is not just a social visit," she said. "I need to ask you to do something very important for me."

"Sure!" At that point, I would have done anything for her, but I was scared that I wouldn't be able to do whatever it was and she'd be disappointed.

"Dad would go crazy if he knew what I'm about to do. I mean, craz*ier*." She searched the pockets of her coat and removed a foil-wrapped sphere the size of a baseball. "I need you to take this and hide it for me."

"What is it?"

"*Stein der Toten.* The Stone of the Dead."

"Sounds cheery." I kept looking at it. It shone strangely because of the foil.

"No matter how well I hid it in our house, Suzie would find it. I need you to keep it away from her."

"What would she do with it if she found it?"

Ilona held it out to me. "Remember the flashing lights?"

I looked toward their attic window, remembering the horror of that night. "Uh-huh."

"That happened because Dad activated this Stone." She pressed it into my hand.

It felt hollow and much lighter than I'd expected.

"What I'm asking you is a *really* big deal. This thing is pure evil and I'd totally understand if you don't want to be anywhere near it."

I looked closely at her face, making sure she wasn't joking. She looked completely serious . . . and seriously beautiful.

"Do you want to see it?" she asked. "You can take off the tinfoil if you want—just not for too long."

"Will a dead lady pop by for a visit?"

"Not if you don't activate it."

I had no intention of *activating* it, whatever that meant. I gingerly peeled back the foil.

"You don't need to be so careful. It can't be broken."

I removed the foil entirely and set it on my knees. The Stone felt like dried clay. It was all different shades of orange, with strange symbols carved into its surface and thin lines crisscrossing the circumference. It looked like it could turn in sections like some kind of prehistoric Rubik's Cube.

I instinctively shifted my grip. I had a sudden, pressing desire to turn and rearrange the sections.

"Don't turn the dials," Ilona said, putting her hand on mine. "That's how you activate it."

Her hand stayed on mine for what felt like a very long while. Then she took the Stone back from me and grabbed the foil off my knees. She tried to rewrap the stone, but the foil split in places, showing the orange stone underneath. She made a face. "Do you have any tinfoil? You need to keep it completely covered in tinfoil at all times."

"I have tinfoil. I'll give you tinfoil . . . *if* you tell me why it needs to stay wrapped."

"To keep its evil power from radiating and calling you to it."

"So, not to preserve it? Like chicken?"

"Harold. This is not like *chicken* at all. For goodness sake." She extended her arm and gave the Stone back to me. "And no matter what, never, ever, ever activate it, never turn the dials. It would make everything go cuckoo-crazy, and then you'd get really sick, just like Dad."

I looked at the symbols through the splits in the tinfoil. Some looked like animals, others like stick-figure humans. "Why would Suzie want to get sick and make everything go cuckoo-crazy?"

"It's Dad's fault. He bought this Stone because . . ." She stopped. "You're going to think we're totally insane."

"Oh, don't worry. I've already come to that conclusion."

She nodded. Apparently, being seen as totally insane was just a side effect of the Goolz lifestyle. "The Stone of the Dead opens a bridge to the other side."

"The other side?" I immediately thought of the

bridge between our houses, but I knew that wasn't the type of bridge she was talking about.

"The Stone brings back the dead. My dad and Suzie want to use it to bring back my mother. My *dead* mother." She stared straight into my eyes. "You have to help me. Now that Dad has promised not to use it anymore, Suzie won't stop looking for it. She won't stop until our mother slides down from heaven and gives her a hug. Only, the more you use it, the sicker you get, the crazier you become, and in the end you die. The bridge goes both ways, Harold. In come the dead, out go the living."

"Oh."

"*Oh* is right."

I didn't feel like making a silly joke or doubting anything she said about the Stone. I had dreamed of having an adventurous life, and now the opportunity was shining in the palm of my hand.

"Will you help me keep the Stone away from Suzie?"

"I'll keep it for you," I said with a clarity that made me feel stronger than steel.

• • •

We went to the kitchen to get more tinfoil. Ilona took my chair and carried it downstairs after I got into the lift. I didn't ask her to; she just did it. I liked that about her. She was never awkward with me. And I never felt like I was special needs when she was around.

Ilona covered the Stone in two extra layers of tinfoil. "Promise me you won't take it out of the foil," she said.

"I won't touch it," I promised. "I'm not big on dead people and Mum will go nuts if I start poltergeisting her precious china all over the house."

"Where are you going to hide it?"

"In my room?" I suggested, though I didn't relish the idea of sleeping so close to it, with nothing but tinfoil protecting me from its dark magic.

"Where in your room?"

"Does it really matter? Suzie won't come in here uninvited, anyway."

"Yeah, right. You saw her at the Owl House. Nothing stops Suzie, ever. And she'll be drawn to it, like a zombie sniffing brains."

She handed me the Stone, apparently deciding she could trust me with it. "Will you keep it on you all the time? That's the only way I'll know it's safe. It can't hurt you if it's wrapped up."

I looked at the Stone. I didn't like the idea of carrying it around, but I couldn't bring myself to refuse her either. She'd come to me for help. So I nodded and slipped it into the pocket of my hoodie.

We went back up to my room, passing Mum in the hallway.

"Still behaving?" she asked, a bunch of files and an empty coffee cup in her hands.

"To the point of pain, Margaret," Ilona told her.

I instinctively put my hand over the Stone in my pocket. I hoped it was just my imagination, but it was starting to feel like a vibrating ball of ice.

Mum stopped at the head of the stairs and watched us as we went to my room. "Harold?" she asked.

I turned around at the threshold. "Yeah?"

"Everything all right with you guys?"

"Yeah, sure, why?" I must have looked all wrong, since I was fighting an urge to grab the Stone and throw it far away from me.

"You look like you've seen a ghost. Wait, no . . ." she shook her hand in front of her face like she could erase the words, "You *can't* have seen a ghost because that would be impossible. Ghosts don't exist and neither does any other kind of monster, in attic windows or anywhere else. Right?"

"Right! There's no such thing as ghosts. That would be like . . . *pffft!*" I disappeared into my room before Mum could ask me to elaborate. I closed the door and turned to Ilona, who was grabbing her coat off my bed.

"You're leaving?" I asked, disappointed.

"Yep," she said, heading toward the window.

"And you're still not going to use the door?"

"Perfection comes from practice." She jumped out like a superhero and I leaned out to watch her climb down. She gave a military salute once she reached the ground, just like I had the other night, and ran back home across the bridge. I was smiling inside and out. Ilona Goolz had a way of making me happy.

But then I looked up at the attic. "Crap!"

Suzie was there, watching me. There was no doubt she'd seen her sister climbing out my window. She waved at me and made the same salute Ilona had, just to prove it. And the strange icy sensation from inside my pocket got two degrees colder.

9

RESURRECTION

Mum called me for dinner. I checked my window one last time, making sure it was locked in case Suzie decided to take that route.

I couldn't stand the chilling sensation of the Stone in my pocket. I had to get it away from me and put it somewhere Suzie wouldn't find it. I chose my underwear drawer. I wrapped the Stone in my Superman boxer shorts, then buried it under layers and layers of underpants and mismatched socks. I stirred up the mess so it would look even messier and added a few T-shirts on top, making one of them hang partway out. I backed away to appreciate the chaos I'd created. It looked like the Bermuda triangle of clothes, and I decided no human being in her right mind would get anywhere near it.

I closed the door on my way out. It was an old door with a keyhole, but I'd never thought about locking it. I decided to ask Mum for the key in case Suzie got into the house from downstairs.

"You'll never get to it," I said to an imaginary Suzie.

An incredible smell floated up from the kitchen. Mum had baked one of her vegetarian pies—she was ace at them. I went to the table and sat with my back to the veranda. Normally, I ate facing the view of the beach, but since I'd seen the ghost lady in the attic, I'd tried my best to avoid whatever hid out there in the dark.

Mum brought the pie to the table and sat down. She took a sip of wine and sighed happily. "We could go to the pier after dinner if you like. Breathe some fresh air."

"I'd rather stay here," I said, trying the pie. She'd decorated it beautifully, with leaves and flowers and vegetables she'd sculpted from leftover dough, and it was delicious, just like all of her cooking. "Hey, do you know where the key to my room is?"

"You want to lock yourself in?"

"Is that a problem?"

"Actually, yes, it is a problem."

"Why?"

She drank some more wine, thinking about it. "What if you fall? Or get stuck? Just close your door. I won't disturb . . . whatever you're doing in there." She blushed.

"That is totally not the point."

"Oh, Harold," she said sadly. "You're changing so much and so fast since you met Ilona Goolz. Though it's a normal process, I suppose."

"What process?"

"Growing up. Wanting new things. Changing who you are."

"I haven't changed."

"Skipping school? That's not you at all."

I didn't want to talk about that. I'd already lost my computer and phone to that conversation. "Will you give me the key, then?" I snapped.

"No," she snapped back.

I was getting frustrated fast. I just wanted to keep Suzie Goolz away from the Stone, but Mum insisted on having this big awkward talk about it.

"Maybe I didn't like who I was before I met Ilona." We were both playing with the pie on our plates, moving it around, but not eating.

Mum stopped fiddling with her food and let her fork drop onto her plate. "*I* like who you are, Harold. You're a great kid. You always were, and you always will be."

"Can I go eat in my room?" I asked, pushing away from the table before she could say no. She sighed and took my plate to the sink. She noticed the roll of tinfoil we had left out, ripped off a piece, and used it to cover my slice of pie.

"Here," she said, handing it to me.

I snatched it, dropped it on my lap, and went to the stairs.

"Harold?" she said.

I stopped. "Yeah?"

"I love you."

"I know," I said, shifting myself onto the lift and squashing my takeaway pie in the process. I held onto my chair and pushed the button. She kept looking at me while the lift took me upstairs.

"I love you, too," I said midway.

"Well, fine, then." Her voice was shaky. She forced a smile and went back to the sink, but I could tell she was trying to hide tears.

• • •

I opened the door to my room, and immediately

86

knew something Goolz-ish had happened while I was downstairs. And it wasn't just a feeling—there were obvious clues that I had been robbed. The most obvious was my Superman boxer shorts lying in the middle of the room.

"No way," I said, going to check the window. The latch was open. "How the heck did she do it? These people are unbelievable."

I threw my squashed pie on the bed and went to the drawer even though I already knew the Stone wouldn't be there. She'd taken it and left the tinfoil behind. I cursed. Ilona had asked me to do one simple thing and I'd failed. I went back to the window to see if Suzie was up in the attic, taunting me with the Stone. It was nighttime, and watching the Goolz's attic window wasn't exactly my favorite activity, even in the light of day.

But I didn't have to. Suzie was walking down the road toward the pier.

"Suzie, where're you going?" I muttered to myself.

I rushed out of my room, then got really frustrated with the slow pace of the lift. I was losing precious seconds.

"Do you want some more pie?" Mum asked from the sofa, where she was reading a Frank Goolz novel.

I transferred my body back into my chair and grabbed my jacket on my way to the door. "I'm going out."

"To see Ilona?"

"No! Just getting some fresh air like you said!" I shouted and slammed the door before she could slow me down with more questions.

I went to the road at top speed, hoping to catch up with Suzie. I decided not to stop for Ilona. I wanted to fix this all by myself. I could get the Stone back, and she would never know I'd lost it. I would keep it on me at all times like she had asked. "Please, please, please!" I begged, speeding from one streetlight to the next.

I was gaining ground on her. I could see her passing the pier and starting down the road toward Newton.

"No!" I said to no one in particular. Because now I had a pretty good idea where she was going: back to the abandoned church. I didn't want to follow her. I didn't want to be anywhere near the Hewitt grounds at night, not with the dogs and Alex and his gun haunting the area. It was the stuff of nightmares. I wheeled even faster. Suzie was a little dot moving toward the full moon. My throat tightened. I thought about going back to get Ilona, but I didn't want her to think I was weak.

"This sucks," I said.

The closer I got to the church, the more I could hear the dogs barking wildly, the sound echoing all around me, as though they could sense a perfect meal on wheels coming straight to them.

I stopped at the church. Suzie was nowhere to be seen, which meant she'd already crawled inside. I smacked the wooden wall with the side of my fist.

"Suzie!" I yelled, knocking hard.

"Go away!" she said from inside.

"I won't go away until you give me back the Stone."

"Tough luck."

I banged on the wall again. "Suzie! Can't you hear the dogs?"

I looked up as something fantastically large and white slid off the roof and took to the sky. My heart froze solid until I realized it was a white owl flying away from all the noise we were making. I started breathing again and banged on the wall harder.

"Suzie!" I barked. "Just let me in and we can talk about this."

"You're too late."

"Too late for what?"

"I already turned the Stone. Lots of times."

"Oh."

"She'll be here soon."

"Who?"

"My mother. You'd better leave."

Honestly, I thought leaving was an excellent idea. "Can you *un*turn it?"

"Can you just go?"

As she said that, the dogs stopped barking.

"This is not good," I said, and suddenly the moon and all the stars switched off. I found myself in complete darkness. It was silent, too. Totally silent. Suddenly, I didn't care about the dogs anymore. Dogs were an ordinary fear and I was rapidly entering an uncharted territory of terror.

"Suzie?" I called. I reached for the wall of the church, but didn't feel anything at all.

"This is SO NOT GOOD!" I yelled.

I put my hands over my ears as an awful sound burst out of the silence—painful, like a dental drill hitting all the wrong spots. And then someone moaned right behind me.

"Suzie!" I shouted.

I turned around. Suzie was on the wrong side of the wall. Whomever—whatever—she had brought into our world with the Stone wasn't in the church. It was out there with me.

"What's that?" I whispered, as a tiny white dot

pierced the darkness right in front of me. Its glow felt warm and hypnotic. It was steadily growing, as if I were moving toward it, or even worse, as if it were coming to me. I put my hands on the rims of my wheels. They weren't turning. The dot was moving toward me—and it was definitely accelerating. It became a ball, the ball became the size of a window, and the window became a door so bright I could no longer see the darkness around it. And then it stopped.

"Suzie, if you can hear me, I need you to say something."

"Say something," my own voice repeated from out of nowhere.

"Who's talking?" I asked.

"Who's talking?" my voice repeated.

"Stop it!"

"Stop it!" said the echo.

"Who's there?" I asked.

"Say something," my voice responded.

I wanted to throw something into the light. I put my hands into my jacket pockets and found my earphones. I hesitated a second, then threw them toward the light. They froze in midair then, *zoof*, the light sucked them in like spaghetti.

"Crap!" I said. But somehow, even though I was still

sort of scared, I wasn't totally terrified anymore. The more I looked into the light, the more it fascinated me, and I found that the brightness no longer hurt my eyes. I searched my pockets again to see if I had anything else I could throw.

"You don't need to cry," said my own voice. "It was a really old chair."

I stopped searching my pockets. "What did you just say?" I asked the light.

"What did you just say?" responded the echo. Only it wasn't just an echo, I knew now. It was something playing with my memories, searching my mind, remembering things I'd heard and things I'd said.

"This is not funny," I said. My wheels started turning, and I rolled toward the light. I grabbed the rims to stop myself, but the wheelchair kept sliding forward, sucked in like my earphones had been.

"No way," I said, twisting around to escape the light. I tried to roll away from it, but it was as if something had already grabbed the handles on my chair and was dragging it with a great force. Like the earphones, my chair froze just before reaching the light. I pushed myself off and dropped onto the dark, cold ground seconds before my wheelchair got sucked into oblivion. I looked over my shoulder. The light was right behind me, and I knew I was next. I started dragging myself away but stopped when a long-gone sensation filled my body.

"This is not possible," I said. I was crawling on all fours.

"This is not possible," repeated my voice.

It felt like rediscovering the taste of a food I missed or a smell I liked. I didn't want to move. Not because I was scared of the light, but because I didn't want this magic to vanish. I never wanted it to end.

"You don't need to cry," my voice said. "It was a really old chair."

"I . . . I have to try," I said. I put one foot forward, and pushed myself up on my legs. I looked down at my feet. "I'm standing," I whispered.

I could feel it, all the sensations of standing up.

"I'm standing!" I yelled at the light, and it immediately sucked me in.

10

DID YOU SEE HER?

"Harold!"

I opened my eyes. The dogs were barking like crazy, and Suzie was leaning over me, shaking me by the shoulders.

"Did she attack you?" she asked.

"Who?"

"Her! The zombie ghost lady. Did she attack you?"

"No," I said, touching my face and then rubbing my eyes. "I don't think so." I looked up at the sky. The stars, the moon, the tombstones, the church: everything was back. I was lying on the grass, my wheelchair on its side next to me. My earphones were there beside the chair, too. I picked them up and dangled the cord right in front of my eyes.

"Hello," I said to the cord.

"Did you knock your head or something?" Suzie asked, snatching the earphones. She set my chair back on its wheels. "Can you pull yourself up in it?"

I looked at my legs and tried as hard as I could to move them, but the magic was gone. "It was just a dream," I said.

"It wasn't a dream. I saw her, too. She came out of the light. She screamed at me. And then she was gone. I *saw* her."

I grabbed the arms of the chair while she held it steady, then lifted myself up and set my bum on the seat before pulling on my legs. "You saw who? Your mother?"

"It wasn't my mother. My mother was beautiful. This one was disgusting, like she was all dead and rotten and falling apart and just . . ." Suzie made a monstrous face, baring her teeth and curving her fingers into claws. "She was horrible! And she attacked me, like she wanted to get the Stone away from me. My mother would never attack me. She probably attacked you, too. You don't remember, that's all."

She went behind the chair and started pushing, jostling so much I nearly fell out.

"Easy!" I shouted. "Let me do it." I took charge of

95

the chair and we left the cemetery under a concert of barking dogs.

"Tell me what happened on your side of the wall," I said, once we were back on the road.

"Didn't you see the lights? You must have seen the lights. They were flashing like lightning and they were coming from outside, from about where you were."

"I saw a light," I said. "It wasn't flashing though."

"It was flashing! I went to the window to try to see where it was coming from. That's when she showed up. She was inside the church with me. Did you see her?"

"I saw *something*. But it wasn't a person," I said.

"She attacked me," she repeated. "I jumped into the hole on the floor just before she could grab me or the Stone. I heard you scream. I thought she'd gotten you. I crawled out to help and found you on the ground all passed out."

I was still lost in the memory of standing up. It had felt so good I wanted to cry. "We better not say anything about all this to Ilona or your father."

"Agreed," she said. "Ilona would never stop yapping about it if she found out what we did."

"What *you* did!"

"Yeah, right," she said and rolled her eyes. "You're really bad at hiding things. It took me two seconds to find the Stone. We're totally in this together."

When we reached our houses, Suzie turned to run inside.

"Suzie!"

She stopped. "Yeah?"

"The Stone."

"Oh." She fished it out of her coat pocket and held it for a moment before reluctantly handing it over. I watched her run to her house. Then I took a good look at the Stone.

"Can you make me stand again?" I asked it. It didn't answer. I dropped it on my lap and went home.

• • •

The Stone was on my desk and I was staring at it from the other side of the room. My bedside lamp lit our strange tête-à-tête with a soft orange glow. *Come and play with me*, the Stone of the Dead seemed to say.

"You're evil, and I know it," I said out loud.

It felt like the Stone was smiling at me, biding its time until I gave in and started turning the dials to see if it could deliver another miracle.

"I'm putting you back where you belong." I nodded toward my underwear drawer. "So don't try any funny business with me."

I moved slowly toward the desk. I knew I was the one turning the wheels, but it felt like I was being pulled toward the Stone by an irresistible dark force.

I grabbed the Stone, breathing heavily, my fingers clutching the dials. I closed my eyes and pictured myself getting up out of my chair, pushing it away, and walking out of my room and into Mum's to show her what a miracle looked like. I remembered the sensation of standing on my own legs in the cemetery right before the bright light sucked me in. It was the most marvelous feeling ever. I felt the dials twist slightly. My fingers had decided to activate the Stone while my brain was still resisting.

"It will bring her back. It will bring back the zombie ghost lady," I said, using Suzie's exact words, trying to scare myself out of doing what I knew I was going to do.

I turned the dials in opposite directions, again and again, feeling an intense sense of joy and relief each time. Guilt was gone. Fear wasn't even a thing. The Stone was laughing now, and I felt like laughing with it.

"Make me walk," I said. "Please!"

I kept turning the dials until they clicked and locked into place.

The orange glow of my lamp grew brighter as the bulb started a high-pitched hum. I tried to turn the dials again, but they were stuck. Now I knew that I had done something deeply wrong. I also knew it was too late.

The hum turned into a hiss, and the light got so bright I had to put my hand over my eyes.

"Oh, Harold," I said. "What have you done now?"

I was clutching the Stone hard in one hand, my fingers cramping around it. I brought my other hand to my ear and closed my eyes as the hiss grew higher and higher until the sound became painful. And then, with a *blop!*, it stopped. I opened my eyes and lowered my hand. The lamp had become a miniature sun, bathing my room in a bright white light, exactly like the one in the cemetery. I decided this was my cue. I pushed myself up. The chair rolled back. I was standing in the middle of my room, holding the miraculous Stone of the Dead.

"Oh, crap, this feels good!" I whispered and *ZOOM!* The entire room expanded into nothingness, then came crashing back and settled into place. I wobbled and collapsed onto the floor like an over-boiled noodle.

The Stone fell from my hand and rolled away. The glow of the lamp had returned to its familiar pale yellow, and my legs were numb again. The fantasy was over. I was back in reality. And reality sucked in all sorts of ways.

I lifted myself back into my chair and picked up the Stone. I knew that the attic lady could show up again, like she had every other time someone had played with the Stone, but I didn't care. My skin was still buzzing with the memory of standing. I held the Stone up right in front of my eyes.

"You are AWESOME," I told it. But it wasn't radiating, or calling me, or smiling at me anymore. Now it felt dead and empty. I tried to turn it, but the dials wouldn't budge, however hard I tried.

"Okay, I get it," I said. "You need time to reload or something, right?" I went to my dresser, leaning down and picking up my Superman boxers on the way. I wrapped the Stone and buried it deep in the drawer of T-shirts and underwear.

But I couldn't keep my eyes off the half-open drawer.

The Stone inside it was the best thing ever. If it could make me stand, there could be a million other things it could do. It could give me superpowers for all I knew.

And my life would be the thrilling, high-velocity ride it was meant to be.

11

I KNOW
WHAT YOU DID
LAST NIGHT

I woke up feeling horribly sick and looking even worse.

"They force you to skip school. They drag you into traipsing all over town at night. And now, what? They give you a cold!" Mum was making an herbal concoction out of plants from our garden and tons of honey. She claimed it could cure death itself.

"The Goolz didn't give me this." I was staring blankly at my cereal, my head pounding and my stomach roiling with nausea, trying to pretend that the curse of the Stone was nothing more than a common cold.

I looked up and turned to the hall when someone knocked on the door.

Mum went to open it, and I caught a glimpse of Ilona on the porch.

"Harold is having breakfast," Mum said, staying firmly in her way. "He's under the weather. He might miss school today—this time for the *right* reasons."

"I'll just share a piece of toast with him," Ilona said, slipping past her. "Cheer him up."

"Hey!" Mum said. "He doesn't need cheering up, he needs quiet." She followed Ilona to the kitchen, both of them walking ridiculously fast, each trying to get to me first.

"Oh, we'll be so quiet, Margaret," Ilona said. She won the race and sat down beside me, giving Mum the smuggest *gotcha* smile ever.

Mum conceded defeat and went back to working on her healing mixture. She started stirring so hard that the liquid sloshed over the sides of the cup and dripped onto the counter.

"Anything you want to tell me?" Ilona asked, her smug smile gone.

I pretended to be too busy watching my cereal get soggy to look her in the eye. "We don't have any toast. We're into Froot Loops right now," I said weakly.

"I need to get ready to meet a client," Mum said,

setting a cup of her magic potion beside me on the table. "Drink up. It tastes as bad as it smells, but it will make you feel better."

Once Mum had gone upstairs, Ilona pushed the cup away, making a disgusted face. She leaned in close and punched my shoulder. "Besides your breakfast routine and your fart-smelling tea, anything *else* we need to talk about?"

"Depends what you already know," I said.

"I saw you and Suzie coming back after the little brat was gone for an hour." She looked over her shoulder, making sure Mum was still out of earshot. "And then I saw that eerie white light in your window. So naturally, I climbed up to your room to see what was going on. And there you were, in the middle of your room, staring at your dresser like you just discovered fire." She leaned even closer. "Is that where you're hiding the Stone? In a dresser drawer? Did you really think Suzie wouldn't find it in there?"

I looked up from my cereal. "You were spying on me?"

"I was about to knock on the window and ask you what happened, but you started to get undressed."

"You watched me undress?!"

"Cheese, no! I left. I'm not a perv and I'm not interested in the male anatomy. At all!"

"The male anatomy?" I repeated. "Can you even hear yourself?"

"Harold, the point is that I didn't give you the Stone so you could use it. I gave it to you to hide it from Suzie."

"She *is* good at finding things."

"And you're *not* good at hiding them," she replied. "Seriously? In a dresser? In your room?"

I shrugged. "There was a ton of underwear over it. It was camouflaged."

"Why didn't you keep it on you as we agreed?"

I pushed the cup even further away. The smell was making my nausea unbearable.

"Suzie is boiling with fever, just like Dad was. And look at you. Have you seen your eyes? You're turning into a corpse!" She put her hand on my forehead to check for a fever. Her hand felt good on my face, even though she was so mad at me. "You're just like them, sick from using that Stone. You know how dangerous that is?"

"I'm fine," I said, but I didn't feel fine. I did indeed feel sort of corpsey.

Ilona took her hand away and crossed her arms tightly over her chest. "Why did you do it? Why did you activate the Stone when I told you not to?"

I was getting frustrated fast. I dropped my spoon onto the table and closed my eyes. Then I opened them and took a good long look at Ilona. "It does things that are unexpected. Things you wouldn't understand."

"Try me."

There was an intensity in her eyes that matched how I felt. As angry as she was, I knew she was the only person I could tell this to. Anybody else would think I was full-on crazy. "It made me stand. On my legs. Twice. When Suzie used it and then when I used it after that. The Stone can make me walk again."

It took her a minute to process what I'd said, then she shook her head. "That's impossible."

"Exactly!" I barked back. "That's what everybody's been telling me all these years. It's impossible. But the Stone, it doesn't know that—it doesn't care. All I have to do is turn it, and it will bring me anything I want."

She stood up. "Harold, I want it back!"

"Did you hear anything I just told you?"

"Yes, and you need to stop using it. I don't know what it did to you or why. But if you keep activating it, it will kill you." Ilona's voice was shaky. She wasn't angry anymore. She was just plain sad, and that was worse. "I want it now."

"It's yours," I said, but the words made my heart sink. "I'll give it back to you if you want. But it's better if I keep it safe here."

"You're not safe with it. It was a big mistake putting you in so much danger. I'm sorry."

"I'm fine!" I slapped the table hard, causing my headache to go nuclear inside my skull. "And I don't need your pity." I pushed myself away from the table and went to the stairs. She followed me.

We went upstairs and Ilona carried my chair again, only this time it felt awkward. I was angry and lost and sick, and I could tell she felt sorry for me, which aggravated me even more.

We went into my room. The Stone was still in my drawer, wrapped in my Superman boxers. I went right to the dresser and grabbed it before she could. Part of it was showing through the layers of blue and red fabric.

"Give it to me, Harold."

I couldn't stop staring at it.

"No," I said, my own voice sounding unfamiliar. I turned to face Ilona. "I'm keeping it. I need it."

"Oh, Harold."

I clung to it harder, knowing full well I was about to experience the full force of her grit.

She lunged forward, aiming for the Stone, and landed hard on my chest. My chair rolled all the way back against the wall. I tried to fight her off, but her hair was covering my face and her hands were moving fast, trying to get a grip on the Stone. The Superman boxers fell to the floor, the first casualty of the fight.

"No!" I shouted. I pushed her away, but I knew I was losing the battle.

When she straightened up, her hands were shaking, but she was holding the Stone.

"I'm sorry I pulled you into this," she said. I glared at her.

She grabbed the boxers off the floor and wrapped them back around the Stone, then wiped her hand off on her coat. Mum chose that moment to stick her head in the room.

"All good in here?" she asked, her eyes on my underwear in Ilona's hands.

"Yeah, we're good," Ilona said. Her cheeks were glowing red and her hair and clothes looked like she had just finished wrestling a monkey. I must have looked exactly the same. "We're good, right?" Ilona asked me.

"Just leave," I said, and she did, practically pushing Mum out of her way.

"What's going on with you guys?" Mum asked once we heard Ilona slam the door downstairs.

"Nothing. Everything's okay," I said, sounding like everything was the opposite of okay.

"That girl just left with your underwear and you look like you've been through a tornado. There's *something* going on."

Mum stayed there staring at me, waiting for me to confess.

"It's nothing," I insisted, rearranging my hair and pajamas. "Can I be alone for a second so I can get dressed for school?"

"You don't need to go to school. You're sick."

"I'm fine now," I said. The idea of staying locked in and Stoneless was suffocating. I needed out fast. "It's your fart-smelling tea," I said, borrowing a phrase from Ilona. "It really disgusted the sickness away."

She tried to touch my forehead like Ilona had, but I shoved her hand away.

"Mum! I just want to get out of these stupid pajamas without everybody staring at me and go to school. Okay?"

"Everybody?" Mum said. "I'm not everybody, and

I've seen your skinny butt before."

"Please," I said, my frustration reaching new heights.

"If that girl hurts you in any way," Mum said, "she's going to have to deal with me. I'm scared of no Goolz!" and she left the room, closing my door behind her.

12

THE
VANISHING

By the time I was ready for school, Ilona was outside waiting for me. I struggled to reach the road, still feeling desperately sick, fueled only by my anger about losing our wrestling match. And, even worse, the Stone.

"Can we be friends again?" she asked. I wheeled toward her, not sure if I should stop or just pass her by.

"If you don't think we can be friends anymore," she said, "I'll leave you alone for the rest of eternity."

I stopped short right in front of her. The thought of not being friends was even worse than losing the Stone. "Yeah, we're still friends," I said.

"Good." She held out her hand and I shook it, like we were back to the first time we met. As we started toward school, I did my best to hide how lost I felt, but

I couldn't stop thinking about the Stone. I felt like crap.

"You're not going to be in this horrible mood all through this friendship, right?" she asked after a while.

"I don't know. Cheer me up like you said you would."

"Okay." She stopped. "Why won't anyone kiss Dracula?"

I could think of a million reasons that it was a bad idea to kiss Dracula. "I don't know."

"Because he has bat breath. Bat breath! Get it? Haha! Feeling better?"

"Marginally."

I wanted to ask her what she had done with the Stone, but I didn't want her to know I was obsessing about it.

"It's very well hidden," she said, reading the question in my eyes. "If you want to find it, you'll have to learn to fly first."

"Story of my life," I said.

She smiled and we started walking again.

"How's Suzie?" I asked, wondering if right that minute she was looking all over the house for the Stone. I hoped she wouldn't find it before I did. As far as I was concerned, I had dibs. The Stone should belong to me.

"Still sick, like you. Not going to school, unlike you. And I know she and Dad started searching the house as soon as I left."

"Can I join them?" I said, only half joking.

She lightly punched my arm. "In your dreams."

. . .

Mrs. Richer's strong dose of dullness made my headache and nausea that much more brutal. I crossed my arms on my desk and nestled my head on top. At some point, I must have started dozing off. Ilona nudged me just as I was slipping away.

"What!" I said, way too loudly.

She nodded toward Mrs. Richer. Our teacher had stopped reading, and it had nothing to do with me sleeping through class. There was a huge commotion coming from the hallway—people yelling, dogs barking, doors banging open and closed, and a general uproar that didn't belong in a normal school day. Mrs. Richer went to see what was going on.

"Oh, my!" she said, jumping away from the door like she'd seen a monster. And in a way, she had. Jonas Hewitt, Alex's dad, blew through the doorway, two of his dogs at his heels. He was carrying a thick plank of wood that looked ideal for beating someone to a pulp.

"Alex! Where are you? You son of a gun!" he yelled, ignoring Mrs. Richer, who was shouting about calling the police. "Where is he, the little rat?"

Old Hewitt was a nasty, red-haired giant with an ogre's beard and a stomach like a barrel of meat pushing against his grimy shirt, the buttons threatening to fly off and shoot people in the eyes. He had an enormous nose, which was particularly red and blue that morning.

"Mr. Hewitt!" Mrs. Richer screamed. "Jonas! School is the *last* place where you would find your son."

He gave her a long, nasty look, then turned and pointed the tip of the plank at the class. "Any of youse see him, you tell him he's gonna pay for killing that dog. You hear me?" He pushed Mrs. Richer out of his way and moved on to the next classroom. Everyone but me and Ilona went to the door to see the rest of the show.

"Did Suzie use the Stone anywhere near those dogs?" Ilona asked. "Like in the Owl House?"

"Something like that."

"Oh, cheese."

• • •

The police arrived, and Jonas Hewitt went. Soon there were dozens of rumors about Alex and the dead dog going around school. The known facts were scarce: the night before, about the time Suzie turned the Stone,

Alex had left the Hewitt grounds with a couple of dogs. He hadn't been seen since, and his father had found one of the dogs near the old cemetery, dead. Some people said the dog had been strangled. Some said Alex had shot it and fled to escape his father's punishment. Others said Alex had been kidnapped, and his dog killed by the kidnappers. They blamed vagrants. They blamed UFOs. They blamed some ancient man-eating monster rumored to live in the Mallow Marsh.

"That woman I saw in the attic, the one who attacked Suzie last night, could she have killed the dog and taken Alex?" I asked as we crossed the athletic field during lunch break.

"Yesterday, I would have said no. Today . . . maybe. If the Stone can really make you stand . . ."

My heart lifted. She believed me!

But then she fixed me with a stony look. "Which does *not* make it not evil. It just means it's even more powerful—and more dangerous—than I thought."

We reached the bleachers, where we'd decided to have our lunch, far from prying eyes and ears. Ilona sat on the lowest row, and I pulled around to sit in front of her. She grabbed my ham and cheese sandwich out of my lunchbox when she saw me wince and look away from it.

"So, thanks to you guys," she went on, "there's a

dead lady going around killing pooches and snatching bullies." She shook the sandwich in front of my face. "You're sure you're not going to eat any of this?"

I turned away. Food was out of the question for what I believed would be the rest of my life.

Ilona had come to school with ten dollars instead of a lunchbox because she didn't understand how a school could have no proper cafeteria. Now she opened the sandwich and threw away all the pickles and the ham, before biting into it and making a face. "Tell your mom not to use so much mustard next time."

She dropped the uneaten sandwich back into the lunchbox and moved on to the slice of savory pie Mum had packed. She was chewing thoughtfully when we saw Alex's gang of bullies coming across the field. So much for our brilliant plan to stay off their radar.

"We're not going to have enough pie for all of them," Ilona said calmly. "You can give them what's left of the sandwich. Hope they like mustard."

"They probably don't. We better leave." I looked around for an escape route.

She shook her head. "We're good here."

Most of the time I thought Ilona's bravery was a good thing. But sometimes, like when a pack of notoriously bloodthirsty bad boys showed up, it sucked.

116

The boys arrived and spread out, sizing us up.

"This is *our* spot," Peter, the supersized bully, said.

"Times have changed." Ilona kept eating, with no apparent intention of moving. "From now on, this is everybody's spot. Right, guys?"

Peter looked back at his friends. They were sizing *him* up now. He had to do something fast. "You're going to have to learn your place here, freak."

"Now, that's wrong, calling people names." Ilona dropped what was left of the pie into my lunchbox. "I'm starting to dislike you. I disliked Alex. And look what happened to him."

"What happened to him?" Peter suddenly sounded way less confident.

"My theory?" she said. "He's gone to a better world, kicking and screaming."

"What did you do to him?" Ronny, the mini-bully, asked.

"What *I* did to him isn't the right question." And she left it at that, turning to face me, as if Peter and the other boys were no longer there. "Is there anything sweet in that lunchbox, other than fruit?"

Peter looked at her carefully. "What's the right question?"

"Oh." She stood up and went really close to him,

117

like a nanometer away. He couldn't back away from her in front of his friends, but I'm sure he wanted to.

"The right question is *What came out of the night and took him?*" She spoke in an over-the-top low voice, channeling a voice-over from a horror movie trailer.

"What took him?" Ronny asked, biting into the bait.

"Good question." Ilona walked over to Ronny.

I never saw those guys so tense before. On a normal day, they would have been torturing us with huge grins on their faces. But that was impossible with Ilona. She was bully-proof.

She turned to me. "Tell him what took their friend and killed his dog."

"Me?"

They hungrily transferred their attention to me.

"You know something we don't, English boy?" Peter asked.

I realized that actually, yes, I did know something they didn't. I wasn't the same boy they used to torture. Thanks to the Goolz and the Stone of the Dead, I had experienced things, seen things they couldn't even imagine. They were still just kids, whereas I had transformed.

"Tell them," Ilona insisted. "Let them know why

they should be afraid in the dark." She winked at me.

"Right." I smiled. I was in the sweet spot where fear turns into rage and rage turns into delicious revenge.

"*The thing that took your friend and killed his dog,*" I said, mimicking Ilona's horror-movie voice. "*It tasted blood . . . and it will come back for more.*" I winked at Peter like Ilona had winked at me.

He looked like his head was about to explode from shock. Everything was getting out of whack for him: his friend had disappeared, and the guy in the wheelchair wasn't scared of him anymore.

"You're gonna get what's coming to you, English boy," he finally managed to say, pointing a shaky finger at me.

Someone shouted and we all turned to see Mr. Turner, the school janitor, limping toward us at high speed. The boys looked relieved to have an excuse to leave.

"Beware, guys!" Ilona called after them as they walked away. "This is going to be a bad night for bullies!"

Mr. Turner shooed us off, muttering all sorts of choice words about kids in general, and especially the ones at our school as he stooped to pick up cigarette butts.

"Harold Bell, you were abso-freaking-lutely great!"

Ilona said as we went up the hill toward the school building, causing pangs of pride to shoot through my entire body. "'*It tasted blood . . . and it will come back for more.*' Ha! Brilliant! You scared the big cheese out of them!"

"That was fun," I agreed, remembering the fear in Peter's eyes with glee. "It almost made me forget that I'm dying inside."

Our victory even brought back some of my appetite. I opened the lunchbox on my lap, grabbed the abandoned pickleless, hamless sandwich, and bit into it. Ilona had been dead wrong—the extra mustard was the best thing about that sandwich. "But we still don't know what really happened to Alex and his dog. Not for sure," I said.

"You're right," she said. Her eyes shone the way they had the moment before she shoved Alex off the pier. "You're totally right."

"About what?"

"We have to find out what happened to him. And we have to do it tonight."

I dropped the sandwich back into the box. I should have swallowed the mouthful I was chewing while I had the chance. Now, it was going to stick in my throat.

13

A BAD NIGHT
FOR
BULLIES

We agreed to go back to the Owl House right after school.

"We should have brought the Stone with us," I said for the gazillionth time since we'd left school. "Nothing weird is going to happen without it."

Ilona was pushing my chair, helping me across the rocky old graveyard as we approached the abandoned church.

"Not happening. No one is ever touching the Stone again, not Dad, not Suzie, and definitely not you," she responded for the gazillionth time. We reached the church and she came around in front of me. "Do you enjoy being sick?"

"I'm not that sick anymore," I lied, holding her biting, beautiful stare. "I feel way better."

"Do you believe me when I say the Stone would kill you? Even Dad understands that." She nodded at the tombstones around us. "Do you want to join them?"

I looked down at my legs rather than at the graves, my frustration mounting again. I believed her. But I still wanted the Stone.

"Harold? Do you believe me?" she asked again.

"I do," I conceded.

"Good." She gently touched my shoulder, then turned to face the church.

"I guess I need to go in there, then," she said, hands on her hips.

I nodded reluctantly. She picked up a stick and used it to clear some leaves out of the hole Suzie had dug, then threw the stick over her shoulder, dropped to her knees, and crawled into the building.

"Scream if you see anything horrifying. Like Alex's body. Or worse," I said as I approached the hole. But she didn't reply.

"Ilona?"

Still no answer.

"Talk to me!"

Silence.

"If anything's strangling you or eating your tongue, just knock twice on the wall."

She knocked twice on the wall.

"Very funny," I said. I went to the back door and Ilona opened it for me.

"Is there anything in there?"

"Yes, an answer to some of our questions."

"Which questions?"

I followed her in and she pointed at what she had found: Alex's BB gun, the one he'd been carrying when he came to feed the owls, was lying on the floor by the altar.

She gave it a little kick. "He's been hiding in here."

"Or someone dragged him in. Or some*thing*."

"So, I have good news and bad news," she said, brushing dirt and spiderwebs out of her hair and off her black dress.

"Start with the good," I suggested.

"We're going to spend the evening together. And since I like you, I see it as a good thing."

"Since I like you too, I think that's a brilliant idea," I said. I was trying to sound cool, but my burning cheeks weren't helping.

"The bad news," she continued, "is that we're going to spend the evening *here*, with that gun, waiting for the thing that took Alex to show up."

The Hewitt dogs had been silent so far, but now they started to bark in the distance. We both turned at the sound.

"Funny," I said. "Sounds like the dogs don't like your plan."

"It's a *great* plan," she objected. "Let's go home, get ready, and prove them wrong."

• • •

Mum agreed with the dogs, though. She thought going out that night was a terrible plan, even after I drank a couple cups of her fart tea and did my best to pretend I felt perfectly fine.

Of course I didn't tell her about the cemetery or the hunt for the missing bully—I told her Ilona and I were going to the beach for a nighttime picnic.

But Mum knew there was something I wasn't telling her. And to make things worse, everyone in Bay Harbor was talking about Alex's disappearance and the dead dog. Mum was completely freaked out and ready to lock me up at home.

"I'm just going to eat a sandwich and watch the

ocean, right there in front of the house," I said, pointing out the window past the dunes. "Nothing bad is going to happen."

Mum started making the sandwiches, even though I told her I could do it myself. She was too nervous to stand still, and I could tell she was fighting the urge to send me to my room and barricade the door.

"I want you home by eight o'clock sharp or I'll come out and drag you home in front of your girlfriend."

"Fine," I said. "But she's not my girlfriend."

I moved closer to the counter. "Can you make a couple sandwiches without ham or pickles? And go easy on the mustard."

There was a knock on the door. Mum gave me a dark look and abandoned the sandwiches to go open it.

Ilona wasn't dressed in her trademark black dress. She had swapped it for black jeans, a black turtleneck sweater, black boots, her usual black coat, and a black beanie to finish off the look. She looked like she was dressed for a bank robbery, not a picnic on the beach.

"You ready?" she asked, standing on her toes to look at me over Mum's shoulder.

"Mum? Are the sandwiches ready?" I asked.

Mum mumbled something about how silly it was

to make sandwiches without ham, pickles, and mustard, and went back into the kitchen to make butter and cucumber ones instead.

"Why so much black?" I asked, pulling my jacket down from its hook by the door.

"To make myself one with the night."

Mum heard that. She sighed and slammed my lunchbox closed. "That's it. I'm coming with you."

"Mum!"

"We will be fine, Margaret," Ilona said, punching me on the shoulder. "We just need a little fresh air and some freedom after a long, stuffy day spent not skipping school."

I zipped up my jacket and Mum gave me my lunchbox. "Eight o'clock! Sharp! Or I'm coming out to get you," she reminded me.

"Absolutely," Ilona said.

. . .

"She's not buying it," I told Ilona when we finally escaped the house. I put the lunchbox in my backpack, along with the flashlight and chocolate candies I'd already packed, and hung the bag on the handles of my wheelchair.

Mum came out on the porch to watch us walk toward the beach.

"Eight o'clock? Seriously?" Ilona said, once we passed the first dune and Mum couldn't see us anymore. "There's no way you'll be back by eight o'clock. This could take the entire night."

Mum had lifted the no-phone part of my punishment in case we were attacked by a bully-snatching thug. I checked the time. It was six o'clock and the sky was already nearly dark. "I give Alex or the attic lady two hours to show up. If I break Mum's rules one more time, she's going to box me in my room till spring."

"Sometimes it's hard to have a father like mine, someone who doesn't know up from down and never remembers your birthday or shows up to a PTA meeting. Sometimes it's great."

"Did you tell him where we were going and why?"

"I said I was going out. He mumbled something about quantum mechanics and asked me to give him back the Stone of the Dead."

"Did you?" I asked, too eagerly.

"Nope," she said. "Hint: if you're about to ask the same thing, here's my answer: No Stone for you!"

I was silent, doing my best to hide my frustration as we took a turn north toward the Owl House, leaving the beach behind.

"I've been meaning to ask," she said. "What about . . . your father?"

"Oh, I never had one of those."

"Is he . . .?"

"Dead? Nope. He just doesn't exist."

"Everyone has a father. You must know that, right? About the birds and the bees and how babies come to be?"

"I know about the birds and the bees, but Mum decided to buy the bees at a clinic to have me on her own. It's always been just the two of us."

"She's an interesting woman, your mom."

"She's cool. I like her."

What I didn't like was the feeling that we were being observed. I stopped and looked back. "Does it feel like someone's watching us?"

"Oh, yes," she said coolly. "They've been following us since we left your house. Didn't you see them?"

"Who?"

"Alex's gang. They were hiding in front of our houses all afternoon."

I turned and looked in all directions, but I didn't see them.

"Don't worry," she said as we climbed the hill

toward the cemetery. "The second something scary happens, they're going to run away screaming. They're just a bunch of cowards."

"Oh, *you'll* be fine. They always go for the guy in the wheelchair."

"Not when he's with his awesome girlfriend," she said.

I suddenly forgot all about ghosts and bullies. I even forgot about how much I wanted the Stone back.

I came to a stop and caught her wrist. "What did you just say?"

She looked at the ground, scuffing her feet in the dirt. It was officially night by then, but I could still see her in the moonlight. I could have sworn she was blushing. "You understand that was sort of a joke, right?" she asked. "The girlfriend thing."

"Well, yeah. Of course."

But something inside of me was performing a happy dance over the idea that she meant it for real. And a deeper part of me was whispering that this was meant to be. That we were always supposed to meet. And then, I realized I'd been staring at her silently for an embarrassingly long time.

"So," she said, "should we go hunt some ghosts,

or are we just going to stay here and be awkward all night?"

"Ghosts are fine," I said, and we started moving again.

"Let's get rid of *them* first," she said, gesturing behind us. We got off the road and she pushed me across the grass of the cemetery. When we reached the edge, she pulled me back into a growth of trees and shrubby bushes that formed a perfect dome to hide in. We waited a few minutes and they emerged onto the road, looking around for us. There were five of them, all dressed in black, like Ilona.

Peter cursed. "Where'd they go?" he said, knocking the tip of a red aluminum baseball bat against the road.

I pulled on Ilona's sleeve. "Baseball bat!" I muttered when she looked down at me. She put her finger over her lips.

"They were right in front of us, and then they disappeared," one of them said.

"We should have jumped them on the beach," said another.

"We need to know what they did to Alex first. Then we jump them."

"Maybe they saw us and they're hiding," Ronny said.

Peter smacked the bat against the road rhythmically, the sound making me wince. "We'll split up and search the cemetery. Whoever finds them calls the others."

"Maybe we should stay together." Ronny sounded as scared by the whole situation as I was.

"He's in a wheelchair, and she's just a chick." Peter used the bat like a golf club to smash a rock. "What're you scared of?"

"You saw how she pushed Alex. She's crazy."

"We're crazier," Peter insisted. "Get going."

They walked into the cemetery, then split up and went in different directions.

This was a tiny cemetery. The moonlight made us easy to see. If we didn't manage to get away fast, they would find us in no time. I looked up at Ilona. She was focused on them, determined and beautiful. I felt something tightening inside me. I had been in this situation so many times: this same pack of guys out to hurt or humiliate me. But this time, I didn't care what happened to *me*. All I cared about was protecting Ilona. I was ready to defy reality and jump out of the chair to strike the first one to come near her.

Ilona pulled my chair back, dragging me deeper into the dome of vegetation, but she made plenty of noise doing so. She cursed between her teeth and fell silent. We held still. I stopped breathing entirely as I heard someone coming toward us, pushing branches aside and cursing when they slapped him in the face. Inside our dome, the moonlight was scarce, but I recognized Ronny when he appeared, holding a huge rock in one hand. He looked at us for a long while. Then he let the rock drop to the ground and put his finger over his lips just like Ilona had. We stayed frozen, still observing each other silently until finally, I nodded, and Ronny nodded back. My throat tightened. Not out of fear or sadness, but out of a sudden overwhelming sense of clarity. Guys like Ronny had no innate evil in them. Most bullies were just weak people standing by, silently supporting the evil of others.

He held up his hand, telling us to stay put, and started to back out of the dome. But as he did, something pushed him back inside.

It was the tip of Peter's baseball bat.

"You rat," he said to Ronny when he saw Ilona and me. "You're going to get it worse than them." He swung his bat and hit Ronny hard on the arm. Ronny fell to the ground, balled up in pain. Peter pressed the bat into his chest, pinning him down. Even in the dim light, I could see the cocktail of madness and excitement on Peter's face.

"We're not afraid of you," I said.

He smiled widely. "Yeah? So why are you hiding?"

He was enjoying all this power and control, savoring every second. He whistled, calling his friends to come see the show. Ilona jumped forward and grabbed the rock Ronny had dropped.

Peter raised his bat in the air. "What're you going to do with that, freak?"

"I'm going to break your skull with it if you try anything stupid."

Ronny had stopped moaning. He lay on the ground, quiet and still, doing his best to become invisible. I kept my eyes on Peter's hand and the bat, tensing at the edge of my chair, ready to protect Ilona from the blow however I could. Peter whistled again, annoyed that no one was coming. "Guys! Here's the party!" he yelled.

The branches moved behind him, and I thought it was the rest of his goons coming to enjoy the show. But then I realized it was something much, much worse.

"It's her!" I shouted. Ice-cold fear squeezed my heart as the attic lady came toward us, pushing branches out of the way with her long fingers. Her face was a patchwork of reflected moonlight and shadows, and her lips twisted into an evil smirk.

"Holy crap!" Ronny yelled, his eyes nearly popping out of his face. He crawled away from Peter, stopping at Ilona's feet.

"She's not going to protect you," Peter taunted, unaware that the monster was creeping up right behind him.

The rock fell from Ilona's hands. Her mouth dropped open in shock. "Ohmyfreakinggod!" she yelled.

"What?" Peter said, finally catching on and turning around.

Up close, she was a nightmare worse than I could have imagined. Her skin was corpse-green and her filthy scarf didn't hide that most of her throat had been ripped away. Her white eyes moved crazily in their deep, fleshless orbits, staring down at Peter with two glowing, silver dots that might have once been pupils.

He dropped his bat, opened his mouth, and let out a sad whimper. I was pretty sure he was peeing himself too. The attic lady lifted her hand, a garland of skin hanging off the bones of her fingers. As she grabbed his shoulder, her dry, leathery lips parted to reveal dark, rotten teeth.

Peter screamed, and then we all screamed. Ilona got behind my wheelchair and pushed me hard. Ronny got to his feet and ran, holding tight to his injured arm. We followed his lead and chased him out of the dome. The branches were slapping me in the face, cutting the backs of my hands when I tried to shield myself. I didn't care, as long as we got away.

Soon we were back in the cemetery and the rest of the gang was running toward us at top speed. Ten minutes earlier it would have terrified me, but I didn't care about them anymore. They must have realized that because they skidded to a stop before they reached us.

"Run!" Ronny shouted.

Then Peter screamed from inside the dome. It sounded like something was tearing him apart. His friends got the message and started running with us.

"Ohmyfreakinggod!" Ilona kept repeating, pushing me onto the road at super-high speed. "Suzie's right. This is a FREAKING zombie ghost vampire monster!"

"Damn right, she is!"

14

ATTACHING DEMONS

Mum was delighted that we were back so soon, but all her happiness vanished when I asked if I could spend the night across the bridge at the Goolz's.

"It's a school night!" she protested.

Ilona had decided we were in way over our heads and it was time to involve her dad. As we zoomed back from the cemetery, we had decided to tell him everything. And for that, Ilona wanted to relocate me to their home for the night.

"We'll be in bed in no time, Margaret. Miss Bell."

"Oh, it's Miss Bell now?" Mum set the last plate she was washing in the drying rack and picked up a dish towel. "Do you know how sly that sounds?"

"Please, Mum," I interrupted. "It's not like I've ever asked you for something like this before."

She gave me a hard look. I struck back with my best puppy dog eyes.

"*Everybody* gets to have sleepovers with their friends," I insisted. "Everybody but me."

"We're just across the bridge," Ilona pleaded.

"Please, Mum," I added.

"He'll be fine."

"I'll be right next door!"

"We've been so good, Miss Bell. I mean Margaret! We haven't skipped school in days."

"You skipped school yesterday," Mum reminded her. She was half drying her hands and half strangling the towel.

"See? Huge improvement."

"I promise, Mum. This is going to go down as the most uneventful sleepover in history."

"We're just going to do our homework," Ilona added.

"We're practically asleep already."

"Stop!" Mum shouted.

We kept quiet for a while. Mum sighed. "Let me talk to your father," she finally said to Ilona.

Ilona's eyes went wide with panic. "My dad?"

"Yes, your dad, the adult in charge of you two if I'm to let Harold sleep at your place."

Ilona looked back at her house through the open door. "Is that really necessary?" she asked. "He probably doesn't want to be disturbed right now. You know. Writing and all."

Mum looked at her sideways. She knew something was fishy.

"Let's go talk to him." She threw the dish towel on the counter, torpedoed past us, grabbed her yellow raincoat, and put it on over her pajamas. By the time we followed her outside she was practically running across the bridge.

I was still crossing it with Ilona when Mum started pounding energetically on the Goolz's door. Frank Goolz came to the door and by the way he looked, all lost and confused, I knew he would do a terrible job putting Mum's mind at ease.

"Dad, can Harold sleep over tonight?" Ilona shouted from a distance before Mum could say a word.

"Who's Harold?" he called back.

"My son," Mum said.

"Your son?"

"Him." Mum pointed back at me.

Ilona was pushing me wildly through the soft sticky sand of their yard.

"Oh. Him? All right," he said vaguely.

"I'm your neighbor, remember? You slept at our place. I brought you cheesecake the day you moved in, and your daughter forced my son to skip school."

"Of course I remember!" Frank Goolz said. "How are you, Henry?" he added when we reached their porch.

"It's Harold, Dad. Harold!"

I turned my chair around so Ilona could help me up the stairs.

"I'm fine, thanks, Mr. Goolz," I said, wincing at each hard knock of my wheels against the steps as we climbed them at top speed.

"Harold's spending the night," Ilona said, breathing heavily.

"Is that so?" he asked.

"Yes, it's *very* important, Dad."

Mum crossed her arms tightly across her chest. Frank Goolz looked at her and did exactly the same.

"Important for what?" Mum asked Ilona.

"I meant, it would be nice. That's all." Ilona made

big eyes at her dad, then spoke to him in German.

Mum frowned. "What did you just say?" she demanded.

They ignored her. Frank Goolz asked a few things in German, and when Ilona answered, he opened the door wide.

"We'll be fine," he told Mum, suddenly clear-eyed and sounding almost normal. "I'm taking care of the kids tonight."

He grabbed Ilona and pulled her into the house. I hurried in behind her and Frank Goolz shut the door in Mum's face.

"Now, tell me exactly what happened," he said.

There was a knock on the door. He closed his eyes and let out a grunt before turning to open it. "What now?" he snapped at my mother.

She wasn't happy. She shook her head, looking at me like she was on the verge of hauling me back home.

"I'm going to be fine, Mum," I begged. "Please."

I knew I was breaking her heart. Ilona was the first real friend I'd had since we'd moved to the States.

"He'll be fine," Frank Goolz said, plastering the fakest smile on his face. "I promise."

Mum closed her eyes and sighed.

"Can I stay, then?" I asked carefully.

She opened her eyes and pointed a menacing finger at Frank Goolz. "You!"

"Yes?"

"Anything happens to my son, ANYTHING, and your fans will lose their favorite writer. Understood?"

"Understood," he said.

"You pay attention for a change and make sure they go to bed early."

"All right."

"Separate rooms! Ten o'clock, tops!"

"Mum!"

We stayed by the door watching her stomp back to our house, moaning and cursing motherhood all the way.

"She's a fine woman," Frank Goolz said, closing the door. "Now," he turned to us, happily rubbing his hands together like a hungry ogre before a large serving of children, "what about this . . . zombie ghost thing?"

• • •

It was amazing how a man who was dazed most of the time could become so sharp at the mention of anything paranormal, such as a rotting dead woman appearing out of nowhere and attacking a boy in a cemetery.

We went into the kitchen, still the only place in their house that had chairs. Ilona made watery cocoa and a coffee for her dad while we told him everything we knew and had seen. I did most of the talking. I told him about Suzie in the Owl House and about seeing the attic lady the night of the flashing lights. I even told him about the light in the cemetery and how I'd been able to stand up then and again later, in my room, when I activated the Stone on my own.

He took out a tiny orange notepad and asked me to describe the ghost in detail. Her face, her height, her clothes, her dead eyes. Her ripped throat and rotting flesh.

Frank Goolz was eating up my descriptions, sketching as I spoke. He was a good artist, too, and ended up with something that looked exactly like the creepy specter that we had seen. He showed the notepad to Ilona.

"That's her," she agreed. "That's the monster."

"What is she? A ghost? A zombie? A vampire?" I asked, taking the notepad from Ilona and looking more closely at his perfect sketch.

"She's not a vampire," he said. "Though a vampire would be nice. I haven't dealt with a vampire since nineteen ninety-two. Time flies!"

"You mean like a real vampire?" I started turning the pages of the notepad. "Oh, crap," I added. It was full of drawings of other terrifying monsters.

He laughed. "Of course a *real* vampire. What other kind is there?"

I stopped on a page where he had drawn a creature with long, twisted fingers and claw-like nails, its half-open mouth displaying horrifying vampire fangs. The monster was dressed in a ratty, old-fashioned suit and staring straight back at me with huge bubble eyes drawn with thick black marker. The drawing matched the description of a murderous vampire in one of his novels down to the last detail. I felt a chill.

"It's all real, isn't it? All your stories are things that actually happened to you guys. You really do live like this, all the time."

"Oh, that's the million-dollar question, isn't it?" he said. "Is Frank Goolz an imaginative writer, or totally bonkers, or do we truly live in a world full of ghosts and monsters?"

"So which is it?"

"All of the above," Ilona answered for him. "Dad's cuckoo, but *nice* cuckoo, and we run into monsters, you know—from time to time."

I had a feeling it was a lot more often than that.

Frank Goolz grabbed her hand and kissed it. "Oh, that's so sweet, darling. *Nice* cuckoo! I'll remember that one."

Real monsters. Real vampires. A real zombie ghost staring at me from the attic next door. It was definitely cuckoo, but I wasn't sure it was nice. Either way, there was no time to dwell on it. Attic lady was still out there somewhere.

"So, what is she then?" I insisted, flipping back to the horrific drawing. "Did you ever deal with anything like her before?"

"Does it really matter what kind of monster she is?" Ilona asked. "She's anyone's worst nightmare, and we need to send her back to hell." She put a plate of cookies on the table. "I made these," she told me.

I couldn't imagine Ilona baking cookies. I tried one. It was awful.

"Well, you know what I always say," Frank Goolz told her. "If you know what it is, it's easier to destroy it." He bit into a cookie and chewed on it happily. "Or at least you know what to do if it bites you: Look for a serum, accept that you'll turn into a monster yourself, or cut off a limb before the infection spreads." He winked at me. I had no idea whether he was kidding.

"We think she's here because of the Stone," I said. "She showed up every time one of us used it, except the time I was in my bedroom, but I think it was almost out of juice. And now apparently she's sticking around."

Frank Goolz nodded. He took his notebook back and tapped his drawing with the tip of his pencil. "That's what the Stone of the Dead is meant to do. It brings the dearly departed back into this world. It also kills anyone who uses it too often. A dead person comes in, a living one goes out. A nice, balanced process, really." He laughed, spitting cookie crumbs on the table.

I forced down the bite of cookie. Not only did it taste like a nightmare, but it turned into superglue once chewed.

"Why did it make me walk?" I asked.

"Well . . ." He put his hand on the arm of my chair and leaned forward, fixing me with his intense gaze. "I have no idea. It's not supposed to do anything like that. But I'll think about it." He leaned back. "Maybe the Stone is even more magical than I thought. No wonder it cost a fortune."

"You should ask for a refund," Ilona said dryly.

"I can't ask for a refund," he responded. "The guy who sold it to me lost his mind and died. You kids have to stop playing with it if you don't want to lose your heads." He slapped me on the back of the head. "Literally. Right?"

I massaged my head where he'd slapped me. He'd hurt me a little, even though he probably hadn't meant to.

"You don't like them? The cookies?" Ilona asked.

I was breaking the rest of mine into tiny pieces on the table, wishing I could make it disappear.

"They're fine," I lied, taking the tiniest piece and putting it on my tongue like a pill. It tasted of rancid butter and cough medicine.

"I put arak in the dough. It's a traditional Turkish liquor," she explained. "That's why they're so delicious."

Everything about the Goolz had to be different, even their cookies.

I swallowed the itty-bitty piece of cookie and rinsed it down with bad cocoa. "This dead woman, why is she here?" I asked. "What did she do to Alex? And Peter?"

Frank Goolz took a few sips of his coffee, thinking it over. "I don't know. Depends on who she is and what happened to her when she was alive. Dead people are often in terrible moods when they are revived. And if they're holding a grudge, they can be a real pain. Did it look like she wanted to eat your friend?"

I remembered Peter screaming and imagined the

attic lady snacking on his face. My stomach turned. "He's not really our friend," I said.

"She's really eating people?" Ilona asked. She bit off a large chunk of her cookie and chewed eagerly. "That is so disgusting!"

She meant eating Peter was disgusting. She adored the cookie.

"I didn't say that." Frank Goolz drained the rest of his coffee. "My point is that we don't know what she wants or why she wants it. But I suggest we find out." He stood up. "Let's go."

This time my stomach dropped. "Go where?"

"You're going to show me the place where you saw her attacking that boy. I'll bring some equipment."

"What about Suzie?" Ilona asked.

"What about her?"

She nodded toward the stairs. "She's still cooking with fever up there. We can't leave her alone."

"And we won't," Frank Goolz told her. "You're staying here to look after Suzie. I'm going with your friend."

"What? No!" She dropped the remains of her cookie and jumped out of her chair. "No way!"

"What? Yes way!" he said, smiling.

Funny that no one asked if I *wanted* to go.

A miniscule part of me was thrilled about ghost hunting with Frank Goolz, but most of me was terrified at the idea of going back out there where the zombie ghost was waiting for us in the dark.

"But why are you taking *him*?" Ilona asked. "Why not me?"

"Because he used the Stone and you didn't." He sounded almost displeased that she wasn't addicted to it like the rest of us.

"What difference does that make?" She gave me a hard look, which stung worse than my fear.

"The users of the Stone are a very exclusive club, darling," he said. "We attract its manifestations like magnets. Your friend was the first person to see that lady in our attic, even before he joined that club. Now she appears wherever he is." He leaned over and tapped my chest with his finger. "I think she's attached herself to you, Henry."

"Harold!" Ilona said.

I instinctively brushed the spot where he had tapped me, as if I could detach her.

Frank Goolz went into the hall and came back with a pair of elegant black leather boots. "Come on, then, Harold-not-Henry! We're going to find out what happened to that boy."

"What if she attacks us?" I asked.

"We should be fine. Well, more or less." He slid his bare feet into his boots and pulled up the zippers. "Tell him, Ilona. It won't be the first time we've fought something from beyond."

I looked at Ilona.

"You'll be fine," she barked, sounding extremely annoyed. "He promised your mom that nothing bad will happen to you. He'll keep that promise. He should be more scared of *her* than any flesh-eating demon." She bared her teeth and lunged at me, impersonating a demon out for flesh. I knew she was just sour that I was going on this ghost hunt, while she was going to miss all the action.

"It's *his* idea," I pleaded.

"By the way, Ilo," Frank Goolz called from the hall. "We might need to take the Stone with us. Could you fetch it for me?"

I tensed and immediately forgot about her anger, my soul lifting at the delicious thought of reuniting with the Stone.

"Nice try, Dad," she said. "But I'm not giving it back." She shot another dark look at me, and shook her head in disappointment at my expression. I must have looked like a puppy that got its bone confiscated.

Frank Goolz came back into the kitchen, wearing a long black coat like Ilona's and carrying an old leather satchel.

"What if I tell you, as your father, to give me the Stone right this minute?"

"What if *I* tell *you*, as your daughter, that I won't ever give it back to you, as we agreed?"

He stared at her sternly. She stared back, even sterner. I looked at both of them, hoping he would win.

But he gave up first. "You're so much like your mother." He slapped me on the shoulder, hurting me again. "You know what that means, old boy? We're not going bonkers in the woods and dying tonight!" And he laughed.

15

GHOST
HUNTERS

We left their house through the back door to avoid Mum seeing us. She would have definitely lost it if she saw him taking me out for another nighttime stroll.

As we approached the church, Frank Goolz was walking a good ten feet ahead of me, pointing his flashlight in every direction, talking excitedly and grinning as I struggled to keep up on the steep road.

He turned around when he realized I was losing ground. "Come on, Harold. Hurry up. She's not going to wait for us all night."

I was happy he finally got my name right.

"Aren't you scared, even a little?" I asked, stopping to catch my breath. "Peter, the last guy she took, he's a big fellow, and he was screaming like she was squashing him like a bug."

"Did you see him being squashed like a bug?"

"No. He was behind a bunch of bushes."

"How do you know he *was* squashed, then?"

"I don't, but I heard how he screamed. And I saw how she grabbed him with her rotten skeleton hands."

He nodded then continued up the road. "All the more reason to hurry up!" he said over his shoulder. "He could be still alive. He might need us to stop her from tearing him apart."

"Do we really want to be a part of that?"

Frank Goolz stopped and pointed his flashlight at my face as I caught up to him.

"Are *you* scared of her, Harold?"

"Only a little," I lied.

"You shouldn't be. There is nothing to fear."

"Two really tough boys have met her. One disappeared. The other screamed his head off. I would say there's a case to be made for fear."

"You know what I tell my daughters when they're scared?" He held the flashlight under his chin, which made him look spooky.

"To return to their coffins and close them tight?"

He smiled. "Close. I remind them that the world we live in is like a story. Like a fairy tale. And that it's fun that there are scary creatures in it, like monsters and demons and whatnots that live in the dark. If there weren't, we would be living in a dull story. Would you want to live in a dull story?"

"I've always lived in a dull story. So far."

"Well, that's over. Now, you live in an exciting story. And tomorrow at dawn, you will be thrilled to tell everyone how you survived an attack by a vicious demon. Story of my life." He laughed, but stopped suddenly, lifting his head like a dog smelling a rabbit. He pointed his flashlight toward the hilltop. "Did you see that?"

I followed the light as he moved it from one side of the road to the other. "What?"

"There!" he said, and my heart stopped. A shadow that could have been our monster flew across the beam of light and disappeared into the dark.

"Oh, crap!"

"Indeed." He stepped behind my chair and grabbed the handles. But instead of getting us away from the apparition, he pushed me at high speed up the hill toward it.

"This is so wrong," I said.

He dropped the flashlight on my lap but didn't stop. "Find her with the flashlight! Don't lose her!"

I caught the flashlight right before it rolled to the ground. "Find her!" he shouted again.

"Oh, God," I said. "Oh, God." I pointed the light forward, hoping she wouldn't jump out of the dark and land on top of us.

He slowed to a stop at the top of the hill. We had reached the cemetery and I was shining the light at the old tombstones. I realized that it was no longer the bumps in the road that made my hand so unsteady. I was shaking like crazy.

"You see her?" he asked.

I tried to speak, but my throat had dried up.

I looked up at him. He was breathing heavily from the run, but he was also smiling. He winked when he caught me staring. "Can't you feel it, Harold?" he asked, his voice a breathy whisper.

"What?" I finally managed to say.

"Her presence. Watching us. Can't you feel it creeping up your spine?"

And suddenly I did feel it. "When you see a ghost, aren't you supposed to run the other way?"

"Bah! Absolutely not. You go after it."

And so we kept going, deeper into the cemetery. "Now. Show me where she attacked that boy. She might be spectrally attached to the area."

I aimed the flashlight toward the bushes where she had grabbed Peter.

"So spooky! It's perfect," he said, steering us toward the dreaded spot.

"Don't we need garlic or a crucifix or something?" I suggested as he pushed me into the dome.

"A crucifix!" Frank Goolz hooted. I had to part the branches with both hands as we moved deeper into the dark. "Oh, come on! You don't fight a demon with symbols and superstitions." He let go of my chair and searched his satchel.

I moved the flashlight around. The network of branches and dark leaves formed a perfect prison. I pointed the light at the ground right in front of me. Some of the thick roots snaking around us looked like they had been scraped with a knife. I imagined Peter kicking off their bark as he tried to escape.

"How do you fight her then?" I squeaked. The feeling of her presence was creeping so far up my spine it was practically strangling me.

"We can start with this." Instead of a crucifix, he took out a huge old revolver. I didn't know what was scarier: a zombie ghost waiting in the dark for the right moment to attack—or someone like Frank Goolz with a gun.

He took the flashlight from me and looked around, pushing branches aside with the gun barrel and shining the flashlight into the gaps. "Show yourself!" he called. He did a 360-degree search of the dome and then sighed. "Why isn't she coming after us?"

"Is that really such a bad thing?"

"Harold, when you go hunting for ghosts, the least you should expect is to be attacked by one. Right?" He dropped his satchel on the ground and held the gun out for me to take. I looked at it like it was poison.

"Just take it," he said impatiently. He shook it right in front of my face until, finally, I reached for it. I took it ultra-carefully. It was heavy, so I held it against my lap, making sure the barrel was pointing away from both of us. He knelt to look through his satchel, then switched off the flashlight and stood up. He turned around. He had transformed into a masked monster with two huge, shining blue eyes.

I nearly tipped over. "Oh, crap!" I shouted.

"What?"

"That!" I pointed to his face.

"Oh, this?" He tapped the contraption. He had put on a pair of goggles made of two thin brass telescopes attached to a metallic mask. They buzzed strangely and glowed with an eerie blue light. He adjusted the telescopes, twisting and turning the many dials on them.

"I see," he said, looking around the dome.

"You see what?"

"Mostly shrubs and plants and plenty of nothing. But it's all very blue."

"What are those?" I asked.

He turned back to me, shining the blue lights into my face. He looked like a demented mechanical insect.

"Best buy ever." He adjusted a dial. "Did you know Thomas Edison built a radio to communicate with the dead? He made goggles to see them, too. These are the goggles. They work better than the radio, I hope," he added, laughing.

He picked up the satchel and walked deeper into the bushes, until I couldn't see him anymore.

"Mr. Goolz?" I called, realizing I was alone in the dark with a gun. "MR. GOOLZ!"

"Yes?" I jumped at his voice and turned around. He had popped his head into the dome exactly opposite from where he had disappeared, his goggles still shining

157

their blue light on me. "What's the matter, Harold?"

"You disappeared!" The gun rattled dangerously on my knees as I gripped it with a shaking hand.

"Yes, and so did she, I'm afraid. I'm sure it was her we saw at the top of the road. And then she just vanished." He switched off the blue light, removed the goggles, and put them back in his satchel. "I'm going to take that back from you, before you shoot someone." He took the gun away and handed me the flashlight instead.

I immediately switched it on, trying to cast away all the darkness and hopefully some of my fear.

"She's obviously not as interested in us as she is in those kids." He sighed in disappointment.

"Why would a couple of bullies mean anything to her?" I asked.

"That's exactly what we have to find out, Harold." He got behind my chair and pushed me out of the dome. The gun in his hand rattled near my face as the chair jumped and bounced on the uneven terrain.

"What's in there?" he asked, once we were back on the cemetery grounds. He pointed at the abandoned church with the barrel of his gun and I turned the beam of the flashlight to it.

"Just owls. And the gun we found. That's where Suzie activated the Stone."

He started for the church. I set the flashlight on my lap and reluctantly followed. When we reached it, he turned and looked back toward the trees hiding the Hewitts' farm at the bottom of the hill.

"And down there?" he asked.

"Dogs and bad people," I explained. The dogs had started barking steadily. I thought their message was quite clear: stay away. "Alex lives down there."

"Who?"

"The first boy who disappeared."

He nodded and leaned forward, squinting into the distance. "That's interesting," he said.

"What is?"

He snatched the flashlight from me and aimed it at a spot in the trees.

"There," he said. "See it now?"

I braced myself for the attic lady, and yelped and cursed when I saw something just as bad instead. Jonas Hewitt was standing at the edge of the trees, looking up at us. He was holding his plank of wood, and as we watched, he started up the hill toward us.

"We gotta go," I said.

"Hold on," Frank Goolz said. "He looks like he wants to talk."

"Old Hewitt doesn't talk. He hurts people instead. And he has a plank."

Frank Goolz switched off the flashlight and handed it back to me. The moon illuminated Old Hewitt as he dragged his heavy weight up the hill.

"We have a gun. I think we win." Frank Goolz hid the gun in the satchel. "Hello there!" he yelled, waving at Old Hewitt.

"What the hell are you doing here?" Old Hewitt yelled back.

"Taking a night walk with my young friend Harold here."

Old Hewitt didn't stop until we were within striking distance. He was breathing heavily from the climb and looked even more dangerous up close.

"No one comes here at night!" It sounded more like a rule than a simple statement. He pointed his plank at Frank Goolz. "I know you. You're that big-shot writer."

"Indeed," Frank Goolz said, adding a funny mock bow. Old Hewitt spat on the ground, just like Alex always did.

"I saw you snooping around. You got no business on my grounds."

"Actually . . ." Frank Goolz searched for something in his satchel. I didn't know what would be worse, the gun or the goggles, but he took out his notepad and pen instead. "I have some questions I'd like to ask you."

"Are you some kind of cop?"

"No, I'm just a big-shot writer, like you said." He put his hand on my shoulder. "Harold? Would you mind switching on the flashlight so I can show this man a couple of my sketches?"

I switched on the flashlight and it shone straight into Old Hewitt's face. He covered his eyes and roared like a bear.

"Sorry!" I yelled, turning the beam to the notepad.

Frank Goolz flipped through the monster sketches, searching for the attic lady. "There!" he said happily. He didn't seem to notice that Old Hewitt's already wretched mood was deteriorating fast. He held one in front of my face. "Is this a good one?"

It did look like the rotting woman, drawn standing behind a rough stick figure who was supposed to represent Peter. I nodded, and Frank Goolz turned to Old Hewitt. "Have you seen anything like this creature walking around your grounds?"

"Creature? What kind of creature?" he said, his whole body tensing toward the little orange notepad.

161

"This is just a rough sketch, I'm afraid." Frank Goolz took the flashlight and lit up the notepad right in front of Old Hewitt's face. "But there might be details that ring a bell. Like the bloodied scarf. Or her hair, maybe? She wears it in an unusually huge bun on top of her head. See the dead eyes, too. And the throat, it looks like it's been torn away. Quite gruesome, really."

Hewitt stared so intently at the drawing, I thought he would fall into it. Frank Goolz watched him carefully. "Would you like to see more sketches of her?" He turned the pages slowly. "Does she look familiar, then?"

Old Hewitt looked up from the notepad, his mouth half open, his eyes full of questions and terror. He grunted and shook his head like a boxer recovering from a hard punch. He slapped the notepad out of Frank Goolz's hand and stepped back, pointing the plank at us.

"You get away from my grounds, you nutjob. You get away now." He turned and walked down the hill, nearly running away from us.

"Well," Frank Goolz said, bending to pick up the notepad. "Did you see the look on his face?"

"He looked scared," I said. "But they're scary drawings."

"They were more than just drawings to him," he

said, switching off the flashlight and dropping it and the notepad into his satchel. "That man knows something we don't." He retrieved the goggles, put them on, and turned a dial. The blue light turned on, the goggles hissing and buzzing as he looked down the hill.

"See anything?" I asked.

"No, they're absolute rubbish. Damn you, eBay, right?" But he kept them on, watching Old Hewitt disappear behind the trees.

16

MONSTER DOT COM

The next afternoon, Suzie was waiting for me and Ilona by the pier, throwing rocks into the ocean. She had recovered from her fever and spent her first full day at school. The only fun part of the day, she said, was when the police came to her class to ask questions.

"Two kids disappearing in two days. I bet this town has never been so happening." She threw another rock and this one skipped across the water. "Did they come to your class, too?"

"They did," I said.

"Did you tell them about the zombie ghost?" Suzie asked.

"Nope," I said. "No one would believe it anyway. Except your dad, obviously."

Suzie threw the rest of her rocks all at once, and dusted off her hands on her jeans. "I'll find it, you know," she told Ilona. I knew immediately that she was talking about the Stone and tried not to look too interested. "I'm good at finding things."

"Dad told you. It's bad for you," Ilona told her. "Do you want to get sick again?"

Suzie shrugged. "Dad's just like me, no matter what he said. He can't wait to activate the Stone again. And neither can your boyfriend."

Suzie was right. Getting my hands back on the Stone of the Dead was at the top of my to-do list. Even if it meant opening the gates of hell and letting out all the zombie ghosts in the entire universe. Even if it made me really sick or turned me totally cuckoo. Even if it might kill me. The pull of the Stone was that strong.

Ilona looked back and forth between us and sighed. "Let's go home."

We walked silently to their house. When we got there, Suzie dropped her schoolbag on the porch and flung open the door, yelling, "I hate school! Never send me again!"

She ran inside, leaving the door open behind her.

"She'll find it," Ilona said, as we went down the sandy path through their yard.

"Where did you hide it?" I asked.

"Told you already. You'll have to learn to fly to get it." I turned my chair around so she could help me up the stairs to the porch.

Across the bridge, Mum emerged from our house. "Harold?" she called, "Are you *ever* coming back home?"

"Hello, Margaret!" Ilona said, waving a little too cheerfully. "He'll come home in a little while."

"I'll come home in a little while," I repeated, shrugging like I didn't have a choice. Ilona and I went inside, and I pulled the door shut behind us. I knew Mum was still out there, steam shooting out of her ears, arms folded so tight, she was probably close to breaking a rib.

"My mum didn't look too happy with us."

"My boyfriends' mothers are never happy when I steal their sons away."

"What do you mean? You've had boyfriends?"

She ignored me. "Dad?" she called.

"How many?" I asked.

She looked into my eyes and gave me the same fake smile she normally reserved for Mum. "Many."

"Many?"

"What can I say? I've traveled the world. A boy in every port."

I blushed. It hurt to imagine she had a flock of boyfriends scattered all around the globe, awaiting her return.

"Haven't you had girlfriends?"

"Of course."

"How many?"

I shrugged. "Plenty. Same as you."

"Names?"

"A girl called Sarah," I said hesitantly. I had known a Sarah when I was in kindergarten in England. She was a cuddly old woman who cooked our meals. She liked to pinch my cheeks and call me her boyfriend, so it wasn't a total lie.

"You're such a bad liar."

"I'm not lying."

She stared at me.

"Not entirely," I admitted.

"Well, *I* was, and I'm a much better liar."

"What do you mean?"

"I've never had a boyfriend, you silly sausage. Never had the time nor the taste for it."

I blushed even harder, but this news hurt way less.

"Silly sausage? Really?" I asked. "You sound just like my mother when you call me that."

"I know. I've heard her call you that. And she's so

right, sometimes you really are a silly sausage."

Frank Goolz came to the top of the stairs. "Oh, Harold!" he said. "Good, you're here. I have things I need to show you."

He came down the stairs barefoot, waving some papers at us.

We went into the living room, which was still a chaos of crates and boxes. Suzie followed with cups of her horrible cocoa, and Ilona added her disgusting cookies. We were home.

"Gather around, kids," Frank Goolz said, sitting on a box and dropping the papers on top of the crate in front of him. "You're going to love this."

We leaned forward and saw that the papers were printouts of old photos.

"Oh, cheese!" Ilona said, perfectly summing up our general reaction. "That's our monster."

"Yeah," I agreed. Last night's chill returned, sliding up my spine as I stared at a black-and-white image of her. "It's her. It's the zombie ghost. Just not so zombified."

Frank Goolz leaned back, a big smile on his face. There was no doubt about it. The photograph showed "our monster," as Ilona had put it, but before she became a grinning, bully-hunting, decomposing body. Her clothing was the same, except it wasn't dirty, bloody, or torn. She had the scarf around her neck, the strange hairstyle, and the same intense eyes, though not yet bleached by death and decomposition.

"Who is she?" I asked.

"Everyone, meet Madame Judith Valentin. She's French, if you were wondering." He laughed for some reason.

"French? Why French?" Suzie said, chewing one of Ilona's cookies and apparently enjoying them as much as the rest of the Goolz clan did. "I don't like the French. They're so weird all the time. It's no surprise she attacked me."

"She was a teacher here," Frank Goolz said.

He picked up the papers and searched through them, then selected one and dropped it in front of us. It showed Madame Valentin standing beside a group of students about our age who were dressed in flashy blue, neon green, and vivid pink. Some of the boys were wearing red bandanas, and the girls' hair looked like curly nuclear explosions. You could see the school building behind them. The picture had been taken at the same bleachers where we'd confronted Peter and his gang. There was a caption underneath.

"*Bay Harbor School, nineteen eighty-two,*" Ilona read.

Frank Goolz dropped another photo on top of

that one. It was another class picture, dated 1983. Our zombie ghost, Madame Valentin, still had her trademark scarf and hairstyle.

"Where did you find these?" I asked.

"Oh, I went to see your mother," he said casually. "And she helped me navigate the Internet and print them out. Lovely woman, your mother. And a true computer savant. She makes lovely cookies, too. And a deadly cup of joe. Boy, she likes her coffee strong!"

I stared at him, trying to imagine Frank Goolz spending time with Mum, drinking her lethal coffee, eating her amazing cookies, and stealing time from her client accounts to go online searching for pictures of our zombie ghost.

"What did you tell her? If you told Mum we were investigating Peter and Alex getting snatched by a ghost, she would never have let me come here again."

"I told her I was researching a long-lost relative of mine. Don't worry, I'm a good liar—I'm a writer!" He laughed. "But mostly, we talked about other things."

"What things?" I asked. I couldn't imagine what Mum and Frank Goolz could possibly discuss and immediately thought it must be me.

"Like most grown-ups chatting over a cup of coffee,

we dwelled on the past and licked our wounds." He laughed again.

I couldn't imagine Mum opening up to this strange man, and I couldn't imagine Frank Goolz discussing anything more personal than wanting to see a vampire.

"What past?" I demanded.

"Harold." He gave me a gentle smile. "The present is where the good stuff is, always. Now focus." He tapped the printed picture.

"What did you search for?" Ilona asked. "'Dead woman with strange hair now a zombie'?" She picked up one of the black-and-white prints and examined it intently as she devoured a cookie.

"Close. A giant man lost it when I showed him these drawings last night. It was obvious he knew her. So I did some sketches of her without the blood and rotting flesh, but with the scarf and the curious hairstyle, and I went around Bay Harbor showing them to more people until I got her name. Then your mother helped me research her tragic story."

"What's so tragic about her, beside this horrible hairdo?" Suzie asked.

"She disappeared some thirty years ago. It was a well-publicized affair. They looked for her everywhere.

Never found her. Never found her body either. And you know what else is funny about her?"

"Yeah," I said. "She came back from the dead, and now she looks like a walking nightmare. *That's* pretty funny."

"Yes, there's that. But she also used to own our house. We live where she lived!" He started laughing again. He dropped another print on top of the last one—yet another picture of Madame Valentin standing beside her students in front of our school.

"Oh, cheese!" I shouted, borrowing Ilona's favorite expression. Not because I was currently inside the former home of a terrifying ghost but because of what—or who—was next to her in the picture.

"It's Alex!" I shouted. "Alex is in the picture!"

The caption read, *Bay Harbor School, 1984*, and yet there was Alex standing right beside Madame Valentin, looking extremely creeped out.

"He's right," Suzie said, pointing at him in the picture. "That's him. That's the boy who disappeared. Only dressed funny."

"And that's the other boy, Peter," Ilona added, pointing at the kid on Alex's other side. She was right. Peter was there, too, looking just as uncomfortable as Alex.

"This is impossible," I said, turning to Frank Goolz. "You can't just drag people into old pictures. Can you?"

"Well, that's not entirely impossible. Time is an elastic thing. But that's not what's happening here. What you're looking at is the genius of genetics at work. Those boys are not your missing friends."

"They are *not* my friends," I said automatically. "But that's definitely them."

Frank Goolz smiled. "That would make a great story, Harold. But these are not the missing boys. These are their fathers." He pointed at Alex's look-alike. "That's the man with the plank. That's why he reacted like he did when we showed him the drawings of Madame Valentin's undead self. She was his teacher. Read the names."

I read the names in the photo caption. Sure enough, Jonas Hewitt and Helmut Donahue were on the list.

"They look terrified," I said.

"Maybe they didn't like school," Suzie suggested. "I always look all sourpuss in school pictures."

"Sourpuss! You're funny!" Ilona gave her sister a gentle punch on the shoulder.

"Or they didn't like *Madame Valentin* all that much," I said, remembering how Old Hewitt had reacted to the sketches.

"Maybe we should go and ask them why they looked so terrified all those years ago," Frank Goolz said, picking up the papers. He stood up and practically jogged to the hall, invigorated by his new plan.

"You met Old Hewitt," I said, turning around. "He's not the talkative type."

"True," he said, zipping up his fancy boots, sockless as usual. "What about the other one?"

"Mr. Donahue?" I said. "Most people stay away from him. Especially when he's drunk."

He picked up his satchel, then folded the printed pictures and tucked them inside it. I was pretty sure the old revolver and the rest of his equipment from last night were still in there. "Let's go meet him. And hope we find him sober."

17

GHOST SHIP

If you were looking for Helmut Donahue, you could always find him at Gilmore's Tavern, or on his boat, recovering from Gilmore's Tavern.

Frank Goolz decided to try the boat first, so we followed him to the docks.

"If he's drunk, he'll be violent. He'll be almost as bad if he's not," I said. "From what I've heard."

"What else have you heard?" Ilona asked.

I talked loudly, making sure Frank Goolz would hear me even as he pulled ahead of us on the boardwalk. "I heard to never engage in conversations that could turn into arguments that could turn into him cracking your skull!"

"People like to spread rumors," Frank Goolz said over his shoulder.

"He's been arrested and sent to jail a couple of times," I said. "Peter brags about it. Like he's proud that his dad is a criminal."

"Dad, can you slow down?" Ilona called. He was going twice as fast as we were.

"Do you know which one is his boat?" he asked me, ignoring her request.

"Sort of," I said. I had seen Peter hanging around the docks before, helping his dad unload fish crates from the boat. "It's one of those over there." I pointed at the cluster of fishing boats at the very end of the docks. I had never gone anywhere near them—running into Peter or his father wasn't my idea of a fun afternoon, and the docks were entirely the wrong terrain for me, with steep steps, and ropes and fishing nets and bits and pieces of things all over the ground between the boats and the barracks. I had to be careful maneuvering through this obstacle course. Besides that, the whole area stank of dead fish.

"When your father wants something, he's unstoppable," I said as we reached the docks. Frank Goolz was already by the boats.

"He's always like this when he thinks there's a book in it," Ilona said, moving a thick rope aside for me.

"You mean he's going to write a book about this?"

"Why do you think he's so excited?"

I looked at Frank Goolz taking notes on his orange notepad and realized Ilona was right. He was gathering information to write a book about our missing bullies and the ghost that took them.

"Will we be in it?" I asked. The thought of it made my heart do a happy backflip.

"Dad doesn't write about us, but you might be in it," she said. "Especially if something really horrible happens to you."

"That's great!" I said, ignoring the "really horrible" part. I turned to Ilona. "Can you imagine that? I could be a character in one of your dad's books."

"Totally. You'd make a great character in a horror novel."

"Why?" I said, losing my smile. "Because I use a wheelchair?"

She shot me a dark look. "Because you're interesting, you silly sausage."

"Can you stop calling me that?"

"Can you stop being one?"

Suzie sighed. "Lovers!" she said, rolling her eyes. She ran ahead to join her father.

"We're not lovers!" we yelled after her at the same time. But Suzie was either too far away to hear or pretending not to care.

"She's a pest," Ilona said, but we were both bright red by then.

"That's the one, I guess," Frank Goolz said when we caught up. He was standing on the dock in front of an old, floating green wreck called *The Donahues' Pride*. He took the folded printouts out of his satchel.

"Mr. Donahue!" he called.

The sun was slowly disappearing behind the hills around Bay Harbor. Black clouds were coming in on a strong wind from the ocean, promising rain and darkness. The boat started to rock gently, creating a melody of slapping ropes and jangling bells.

"He's probably at the tavern," I said when there was no answer. As I said it, a loud *THUD*, like something really heavy falling, came from inside the boat as it started rocking harder on newborn waves.

"Mr. Donahue!" Frank Goolz insisted. "This is important. It's about your son."

"Maybe he's passed out," I said, and we all listened for a while until the thudding thing thudded again.

"Mr. Donahue?" Frank Goolz called again. "I'm coming on board!"

"If you brought your revolver, this would be a good time to take it out," I said. "Helmut Donahue has sent people to the hospital just for looking at him the wrong way."

"I'll be fine," he said, stepping down onto the deck of *The Donahues' Pride*. Suzie jumped down after him and Ilona stayed with me on the dock.

Frank Goolz knocked hard on the wooden frame of the cabin, calling for Donahue. He turned to us. "I'm going in."

"I don't have my phone with me," I said. I hadn't been home to retrieve it since we left school. I had no way of calling 911 if Mr. Donahue jumped out of the cabin and attacked us with a giant rusty hook.

I turned hopefully to Ilona.

"I don't own a phone," she said. "Never have."

Another thud came from inside.

"We don't need phones. If it comes to that, I'll follow your excellent suggestion about my old friend in here." Frank Goolz tapped his satchel and winked at me.

"We'll wake him up gently," Suzie said, following her father into the cabin.

I couldn't believe he would drag Suzie into this

with him. Mum would be so mad to see how reckless he could be with his daughters. I looked up at Ilona. "Did you know he has a gun in that satchel?"

"Of course," she said. "These are dangerous days. A gun can come in handy."

"Yeah," I said, trying to channel her coolness.

"Relax," she said, so I knew I wasn't doing such a great job. "He's used to stuff like this." She patted my shoulder.

I felt a little better, mostly because Ilona let her hand linger on my shoulder, and it was nice. And then I realized how long we'd been waiting.

"Mr. Goolz? Everything good in there?" I called. I looked up at the sky as the first drops of rain began to fall.

Ilona's hand left my shoulder. "I should go on board and check on them."

"I can't come with you," I said.

"I'll be fine," she said. She was about to step on board when her sister wobbled out of the cabin, looking pale and seasick.

"Did you find him?" I asked.

It took Suzie a while to focus on me. "No. Dad wants me out of there."

Ilona helped her out of the boat. "Are you all right?"

"No!" She sat down on the wet edge of the dock. "Far from it."

"What's wrong?" I asked, sensing I wouldn't like her answer.

"There's blood everywhere," she said.

"Blood?" I shouted, grabbing my wheels like that was code for "Let's get the heck out of here."

Suzie was turning from chalk-white to pea-green. "I don't like looking at blood."

"Mr. Goolz!" I shouted. No answer. I turned back to Suzie. "What's going on in there?"

"There was a huge barrel rolling around in the blood. That's what was making all that noise. But Dad fixed it."

"What's he doing now?"

"Searching."

"Searching for what?"

"Whoever bled like that," she said weakly, "or whatever's left of them."

"MR. GOOLZ!" I shouted.

Ilona squatted beside her sister. "Just breathe calmly."

"Okay," Suzie said, but instead, she leaned over and vomited into the water.

Ilona rubbed her back gently, telling her everything was going to be fine. But nothing was fine. And things were getting worse—suddenly it began to rain, hard. Ilona helped her sister stand up and we retreated toward the barracks.

"Why is your dad still on the boat?" I asked once we were out of the rain.

Ilona helped Suzie sit on a crate that was lying against the wall and came to stand by me. We looked back at the boat. There was no sign of Frank Goolz, and the rain and wind made the situation even scarier.

"I'm going to get him," Ilona said. This time, she didn't let me stop her. She ran through the rain to the boat, ignoring me when I called her name.

"Oh, no," Suzie said.

"What? Are you going to be sick again?"

She lifted her sneaker to show me a shiny red smear of blood on its white sole. I didn't like the sight of blood either. She leaned sideways and barfed again. I went to her and tried to hold her hair back like her sister had. I rubbed her back with my other hand, but I was pretty sure it didn't help. I watched the boat through the heavy rain, hoping Ilona and her father would come back soon.

Suzie looked up at me. "Go get Ilona, please," she begged. She was breathing heavily and leaning sideways, a couple ticks away from fainting and falling off the crate.

"I can't leave you alone. You look really sick."

"Harold, please go get her. I need Ilona. Now."

"Okay," I said reluctantly. I started toward the boat, pulling up the hood of my jacket and trying to detach myself from my fear. I stopped at the edge of the barracks. Rain streamed from its roof, creating a waterfall. But that wasn't what had stopped me. There was a strange noise, like some kind of thick sludge slowly drip-drip-dripping. Then I caught a glimpse of something out of the corner of my eye and I knew I was in trouble.

The door to the barracks was open, blowing back and forth in the wind.

"What now?" I said, my throat tightening. "A sea monster?"

I headed for the door to look inside. The closer I got, the more obvious it became that it wasn't the rain making that horrible noise. It was something inside the barracks. "Hello!" I called. "Anybody in there?"

There was no answer.

"What's that noise?" Suzie asked. She was back on her feet, but pale as a pill.

I went through the door and froze.

"What?" Suzie said. She came in behind me. Then she turned to where I was looking and screamed.

I screamed, too.

Ilona and her dad came running from the boat.

"What's wrong?" Ilona yelled.

"We found Donahue," I said, looking away. At my side, Ilona covered her mouth and hid her face against her father's chest.

He was in a large glass tank, underwater, with live crabs crawling all over his body and face, his eyes wide, his mouth open in a silent scream, dead as a fish on a hook.

18

A CRY
IN THE
MARSH

We finally ended up at Gilmore's Tavern, where Frank Goolz called the police. There was no police precinct in Bay Harbor, so a few police cars came from Newton and we directed them to what was left of Donahue. Some of the officers stayed on the dock waiting for the coroner and the others drove us to Newton. I was in my own police car and the officer who was driving asked at least once every mile if I was all right. The Goolz traveled together in a separate police car.

The officer was all sorts of sorry that the precinct wasn't equipped for someone like me. She had two of her colleagues carry me up the stairs in my chair. Then we went into a meeting room, where I was reunited with the Goolz.

All of the officers were very nice to us. A younger officer came up and told Frank Goolz he was a big fan; the woman who drove me brought coffee for him and bottled water for the girls and me. She asked me to write down my home number so she could call Mum and tell her where I was.

"She's going to lose it when you tell her what happened," I warned.

"I'll make sure she doesn't worry." She took the sheet of paper with Mum's number. "Trust me. I deal with worried parents all the time."

"Thank you," I said, but the officer had no idea what she was in for. Finding the dead body of Helmut Donahue and ending up in the police precinct in Newton was the beginning of the end of my relationship with the Goolz.

"Let me do all the talking," Frank Goolz said once we were alone. I wasn't sure it was the best approach. I thought Ilona would make a much better ambassador for our strange crew.

"Do you still have your gun in your bag?" I asked.

He put his finger across his lips and winked at me. "No one needs to know that."

"I'm pretty sure you can't bring a gun into a police station."

"It's an antique," he said, as if carrying a loaded weapon was all right if it belonged in a museum.

A short, bulky, bald man in a blue shirt and tie knocked on the open glass door. He was middle-aged, with a funny blond-and-gray moustache.

"Get some cookies for the kids," he said over his shoulder as he came in, carrying a cup of coffee in one hand and a blue file in the other.

He shook hands with Frank Goolz and introduced himself as Bruce Miller. "I'm a big fan. I loved that *Curse* thing," he said. "What was it called? *The Curse of the Dead*, right?"

"That's the name of the TV series. The book was called *The End of Everything*."

"You got me there." Officer Miller laughed and sat down in front of us. He set the file on the table. "I saw it on TV. I don't read much. But still, I liked it. Scary stuff."

He opened the file and made all sorts of noises as he read through it—sighing, grunting, tapping nervously on the table.

"This is a pretty good horror story, too," he said, looking up at Frank Goolz. "What were you doing on the docks, anyway?"

"Researching."

"Researching what?"

"My next book."

"Does your next book involve a dead man in a crab tank?"

"Maybe," Frank Goolz said thoughtfully. "It's an exciting scenario for a story, don't you think?"

"Helmut Donahue might disagree with you on that one."

"I guess he would."

The younger officer apparently couldn't find any cookies. The best he could do was a few tiny bags of chips, which he dropped on the table. But we didn't touch them. I wasn't about to eat anything and I didn't think Suzie and Ilona were either. All I could think about was crabs and dead people.

"And you, son?" he asked me.

"Me?"

I didn't want to answer any questions. I wanted Frank Goolz to deal with everything, like he'd said he would.

"Why were you on the docks with Mr. Goolz?"

"Like he said. Research for his book."

He turned back to Frank Goolz. "You always do your research with a bunch of kids?"

"My daughters are always with me. Harold is new to our outfit."

"And you know him from where?"

"He's our neighbor. He's a nice kid."

"We didn't know we would find a dead man," Suzie said abruptly.

The officer leaned closer to her. "But you were looking for *something*," he pressed.

"Not a dead man," she said.

"What *were* you looking for?"

Ilona and I turned to Frank Goolz, hoping he would intercede, but he was watching Suzie with interest.

"A ghost," she said.

"A ghost?" That was clearly not the answer the officer expected.

"It's for a story!" Ilona blurted before Suzie could say more. "*Obviously.*"

"It's for my next novel," Frank Goolz agreed, putting his arm around Suzie and squeezing her into silence. "We needed to talk to Mr. Donahue about a teacher who disappeared years ago. We found him dead. It was a complete accident."

"It wasn't an accident," Officer Miller said. "His boat was the scene of a terrible fight. He must have weighed more than three hundred pounds, and yet someone had the strength to carry his body out of the boat, lift him up, and dump him into a crab tank."

"Dad meant it was an accident that we found him dead with the crabs," Ilona said.

Suzie turned pale and clapped her hand over her mouth. "Stop! You're making me sick!"

"Sorry, kid." The officer closed the file and leaned back in his chair to take a good look at us.

"A famous writer, two missing kids, a dead body, and a ghost." He crossed his arms and laughed. "Bay Harbor isn't the quiet little town it used to be."

. . .

The officer who brought the chips came back in with a digital recorder. The police made Frank Goolz tell them everything that had happened on the docks all over again. He made it sound like an innocent jaunt— nothing more than a fun field trip to help with a novel he was working on. He didn't mention the Stone of the Dead or our encounters with a real ghost. He carefully left out our search for the missing kids too. I didn't think they were accusing us of anything. And the mood was pretty friendly.

Until Mum arrived.

"YOU!" she yelled, pointing a menacing finger

at Frank Goolz as she entered the conference room. I thought for a second that she was going to hit him. Instead, she grabbed my chair and started to drag me away from the Goolz. She was so angry she was shaking and knocking me against chairs so hard that my teeth clattered. I'd never seen her so furious.

Officer Miller stood up. "Ma'am, you need to calm down." He started moving chairs out of her way.

"I am as calm as can be!" she shouted. "And you!" She turned back to Frank Goolz, pointing her finger at him again. "You and your daughters, you stay away from Harold. Stay away from him. Do you hear me?"

"Mum," I said as calmly as I could. "It's all right. They haven't done anything wrong."

"You stay away from him!" she yelled again, and rushed to the door. Officer Miller tried to stop her.

"Move out of my way," she said and he did, probably deciding it was better to let the madwoman go. Mum pushed me down the hallway at a sprint. I had expected her to be mad, but I hadn't expected her to be *crazy* mad. I kept quiet, even when we came so close to running into a man that he had to jump out of the way.

Outside, it had stopped raining. There was no moon, no stars, just pure darkness beyond the streetlights. Mum pushed me to the edge of the steep stairs. It would be a real struggle to get me down on her own, and she knew it.

"Crap!" she yelled.

"Mum, calm down," I said. My voice was shaking badly and my own anger was starting to build—partly because she had said I could never see the Goolz again and partly because of the humiliating show she had put on in front of all those people.

The officer who had driven me to Newton came out with the one who had brought us the chips. They each took a side of my chair, without saying a word. Mum didn't say a word either; she just followed them down the stairs. They put me down ultra-carefully when we reached the sidewalk.

"You'll be all right, Harold," the female officer said and gently patted my shoulder. "Ma'am," she added, giving a polite nod to my mother. We watched them climb the stairs and go back into the building. I felt my throat tightening. I wanted to cry for some reason. Mum didn't even thank them for their help. We didn't speak as we went to the car. We didn't speak as I got into the front seat and she loaded my chair into the back. We didn't speak as we drove away. I had actually decided to never speak to her again. This eternal vow lasted about three minutes.

She was gripping the steering wheel so tightly that she must have gotten a cramp because she let go with one hand and shook it out.

"We're going to go back to how we lived before those crazy people moved next door," she said.

We left Newton and took the highway through the Mallow Marsh. I tried to keep quiet. I tried to lose myself in the dark landscape, but it didn't work. All the anger and frustration that had been building inside me came up like lava from a volcano.

"I hated the way we lived before they moved next door!" I yelled at the top of my lungs. "I hated our life!"

"No, you didn't," she said, as though she had the right to decide what my true feelings were. And that only made me angrier.

"Yes, I did. Everybody has treated me like I'm a problem since I fell out of that tree. Everybody! But the Goolz don't."

"Calm down," she said, suddenly forgetting her own anger. "We'll talk about this later."

"My life sucks! *Your* life sucks because of me. Look at me!"

"We are absolutely fine," she said, keeping her eyes on the small portion of the road that our headlights dragged out of the darkness.

"I'm trapped forever in this stupid body," I said, yanking at my jeans.

"Harold, you stop this right now. You are not trapped."

I had never talked like this. I had never complained about the unfairness of what had happened to me just because I wanted to grab a stupid plum out of that stupid tree. And Mum obviously didn't want me to start now. But the more she resisted it, the more I wanted to dig till it hurt.

"I wish I died that day," I said.

She hit the brakes and jerked the car off the road, nearly driving us into the marsh. Several cars veered around us, blaring their horns and flashing their headlights.

Mum didn't care. "You are my everything!" she said. I could see tears running down her face in the dim light of the dashboard.

Tears started running down my face too. I wiped them away fast.

"My life with you does not suck. My life with you is the best thing that I ever could hope for, and I'm not going to let a lunatic writer and his two spoiled daughters take that away from me."

We sat in silence, staring out at the marsh. There was just enough moonlight to see the high grass moving in the wind. Then Mum spoke.

"Harold, look at me, now."

I did.

"You are my favorite person in the world." She put her hand on my face and her touch felt surprisingly nice. "You are never a problem. You are my solution. You got that?"

I nodded. Words wouldn't come out anyway. I was out of anger. It had passed, for both of us, and we were back to what we'd always been: a unit of two on our own on this planet. She let go of my face and gave me a little tap on the head. "There!" she said, as if that silly tap was my punishment. And then she started the engine and drove away.

19

GONE
WITH THE
DARK

But the tap on my head was far from the end of it. A complete Goolz embargo went into effect. Valid indefinitely.

"I'm going to blow up that bridge with dynamite," Mum said as she threw her yellow raincoat onto the sofa. She sounded dead serious.

I went up to my room and straight to the window. I instinctively looked up at the little round attic window, but it was dark and empty. And then, I waited for the Goolz to return.

I was about to give up when a police car pulled up to their house and the three of them climbed out. Frank Goolz stayed by the car, talking to the driver. I thought I recognized Officer Miller behind the wheel, but I couldn't be sure. Ilona looked up and waved at me as she and Suzie walked to their house. I waved back and immediately felt that the world was right again.

Frank Goolz knocked on the hood of the police car and it drove away. He waved at me too before he went into the house. Mum was right. She would have to blow up that bridge to keep me away from the Goolz. Ilona had been absolutely right about needing a secret route to my room. I was sure she would climb up any minute so we could recap the day's morbid adventure on the docks.

I picked up *Voodooland* and started reading on a random page. It felt different now that I knew the truth. It felt magical. I looked out the window again.

Frank Goolz was stepping out his front door. He had his satchel with him, meaning he was up to his usual tricks. Ilona and Suzie followed him onto the porch and stopped there. When Frank Goolz reached the middle of his yard, he paused and looked up at me. He searched his satchel and took out his goggles, then put them on and shot their eerie blue light straight at me. He gave me a thumbs up. I didn't know if he was trying to be funny or he'd seriously just checked for a ghost beside me in my bedroom. He removed the goggles, put them back in his satchel, and walked away toward the pier, which was also the way to the old cemetery.

"Where is he going?" I said as loudly as I dared, looking down at Ilona. She shrugged like she either didn't know or didn't understand what I was asking.

Whatever ghost expedition Frank Goolz was going on, he wanted his daughters to stay safely out of it. Ilona said something, but I couldn't hear her either. I unlocked the window and opened it as discreetly as I could.

"What?" I whispered.

"Your mom is watching us," she said, pointing at our house.

"Oh." I looked down and saw Mum's shadow projected across the yard in the light from our kitchen window. I imagined she'd seen Frank Goolz doing the goggles trick, too, which I was sure made her desire for dynamite even stronger.

"Right," I said, closing my window.

Ilona mouthed something else. I was pretty sure she'd said, "See you later," so I gave her a thumbs up just like her father had and watched her go back inside with Suzie.

• • •

I went back to reading *Voodooland*, though I couldn't really focus on it. I was waiting for Ilona to come knocking on my window. Eventually I fell asleep and dreamed that I was trapped in a mall, trying to find an elevator that wasn't out of service. I woke to a touch on my shoulder.

"Crap!" I said when I opened my eyes to find Ilona sitting on the edge of my bed. "When did you get here?"

She shrugged. "Just now." The window was open behind her and the wind played with her hair.

"What time is it?" I asked.

"Almost midnight."

She leaned over me and switched off my bedside lamp. The sky had cleared and the moon provided us with all the light we needed.

"Dad hasn't come back," she said.

"Where did he go?"

"He went to see Alex's father. Dad's sure that man holds all the missing pieces to this puzzle."

"He also holds a plank of wood that could crush your dad's head."

"I know," she said, taking my hand. She held it silently and I liked that very much.

"I gotta go, Harold."

"Go where?" I already knew the answer; I just didn't like it.

"I have to go look for Dad."

"Where? The Hewitt grounds? In the middle of the night?"

Her silence was my answer.

"Let's call the police and get them to go," I suggested. I didn't want to let go of her hand. We'd been holding hands for so long now that it felt like it meant something.

"We can't do that," Ilona said.

"Why not?"

"We have no idea what's happening or what Dad's up to. We need to find out before calling in the cavalry."

"I can't go with you," I said. "I can't go down the stair lift without waking Mum up and if we wake her up trying to go on a midnight hunt, she will kill the both of us and then your dad."

"I didn't come up here to ask you to come with me," she said.

"No?"

"I came up here because I wanted to do something else." Her face was really close to mine. She erased the space between us and kissed me on the mouth.

"Why did you do that?" I asked when it ended.

"Cheese, Harold. Use your imagination." And she did it again. I sort of lost myself in that second kiss. I didn't know if she was a good kisser. I didn't know if I was a good kisser either—I'd never kissed a girl before. But I liked it and I still wanted more when she stopped and let go of my hand.

"I gotta go." She stood up and backed away from my bed.

"Wait." I didn't want her to go anywhere, but I couldn't think of a good reason to make her stay. I grabbed my phone from the bedside table. "Take it. You can call the police."

She came back. She grabbed my phone and I caught her hand.

"I gotta go," she repeated, gently pulling away.

I thought I was supposed to tell her something deep and meaningful to let her know how much I cared for her. "One, two, three, four," I said, instead.

"What?"

"It's the pin number for my phone."

She smiled. "One, two, three, four," she repeated and dropped my phone in her coat pocket. She left through the window.

I dragged myself into my chair and went to the window. Suzie was waiting for her on their porch. Ilona showed her my phone. Suzie looked up at me, but she didn't wave. I had a feeling she knew something had happened between Ilona and me besides borrowing a phone. I watched them walk away toward the pier. I stayed by the window long after they were out of sight.

. . .

"Calm down," I said to myself, checking the time on my stormtrooper clock. It was nearly two a.m. and the Goolz were still gone.

"They're fine. She has your phone. Frank Goolz has Indiana Jones's revolver," I told my own reflection in the window. It didn't help. I looked up at their attic. Madame Valentin's ghost wasn't at home either. Or if she was, I couldn't see her. All I could think about was Old Hewitt and his plank of wood, Donahue in the fish tank, and the way Ilona had kissed me before she left.

"Do something!" I ordered my reflection. I went into the hallway. The boards under my wheels creaked up a storm. I could hear Mum snoring through her wide-open door. I considered waking her up to tell her about the missing Goolz. I knew it was a terrible idea, but going back to my room and doing nothing wasn't much better. I couldn't take it any longer. I *needed* to know what was going on. I approached the lift. It made so much noise, it would definitely wake Mum if I used it. At that point, I just wanted to get to the phone downstairs to call Ilona. I slid onto the lift and threw down my chair. It bounced down the stairs, making tons of noise, then landed on its wheels and rolled all the way to the hall. I stayed on the second floor in the lift, listening. Mum had stopped snoring. I was sure she'd come out to investigate, but she started snoring again instead. I had my hand on the lift remote. My chair was already downstairs. If I could go down without waking Mum, and somehow get back into my chair, I might be able to avoid capture.

"This is going to hurt," I muttered. I let go of the remote and pushed myself off the lift, aiming for the hallway. I crash-landed with the grace of an oversized hippo. Mum stopped snoring again and I heard her twisting and turning in bed. I stayed put, holding my breath. She stopped moving, spoke a few indiscernible words, and started snoring once again. So far, so good, I thought, and started crawling down the stairs like a disarticulated ghost in a Japanese horror movie. It was the first time I had done this, and I aced it, going at the exact right speed to keep my feet from drumming on the steps. I made it downstairs, crawled to my chair, and lifted myself into it. I could hear Mum snoring even from the bottom of the stairs. I was pretty proud of myself. I totally ninjaed that thing. I went to the phone in the kitchen and dialed my own number. The phone rang and rang until my voicemail came on. I tried again and this time left a message: "Answer me, please," I whispered. "I'm worried."

I hung up. I was sure Ilona was in trouble and I didn't know what to do. I dialed the first digit of 911, but then hung up. Calling the police felt wrong. What could I tell them? My neighbors went for a night walk and didn't come back, but we should be alarmed because there was a zombie ghost running around feeding people to crabs?

A wave of panic flowed through me as I thought of Donahue inside the tank. I couldn't stay like this, waiting for something to happen. I thought of Ilona holding my hand up in my room.

"I have to know," I whispered.

I had left my jacket in my room, so I unhooked Mum's yellow raincoat and put it on. Her secret pack of cigarettes was in the pocket. I smiled and shook my head. "Busted," I muttered.

I opened the door as silently as I could and went out. My keys were in my jacket in my room and I had

no idea where Mum had put hers. I didn't want to lose
any time searching for them, so I left the door unlocked
for when I returned safe and sound.

How naïve of me.

20

NIGHT TERROR

Best-case scenario: Frank Goolz and his daughters were walking around the old cemetery looking at things with his funny goggles. Worst-case scenario: they were running through the woods to escape a madman with a plank of wood or a decomposing ghost with a thing for crabs. And I was on my way to join them, armed only with a yellow raincoat and a pack of cigarettes. No phone. No flashlight. No revolver. No goggles.

"I hope Madame Valentin likes to smoke," I said to myself as I approached the old cemetery. I struggled to roll between graves to reach the church and knocked on the wall above the hole Suzie had created to get in.

"Ilona? Suzie? Are you in there?"

Something moved inside. I knocked again and a

large white shape flew off the tower. I had scared off an owl. It flew down toward the trees around the Hewitt grounds. The dogs were unusually silent. I didn't like not hearing them barking. It reminded me of the night Suzie had used the Stone inside the church. It reminded me of all the horrific sightings of Madame Valentin.

I moved away from the church, crossed the cemetery, and got back on the road, then stopped to listen, doing my best to ignore my fear. Nothing moved. Nothing attacked. Nothing howled at me from the darkness.

"Thank you," I muttered in case the ghost of Madame Valentin was listening. "I'll ignore you and you won't eat my face. Deal?"

I went to the top of the hill and looked down at the thick patch of trees. I was starting to think I'd never find them when a blue light cut through the darkness.

"Oh, thank God," I said. I blessed the sight of Frank Goolz's silly goggles. He was down there, and he and the girls were probably fine. I thought of going down to meet them, even though I knew it could be a one-way trip for me, as it was way too steep to come back up without help. But then a dog barked. I froze. Others joined in, yapping angrily. The two tiny dots of the goggles turned toward me. I waved. I must have been easy to see, in my bright yellow. The blue dots moved

207

away from me and emerged from the woods—but not on Frank Goolz, on a huge bearded creature, holding three dogs on leashes in one hand and brandishing a plank of wood with the other. The dogs went wild as they approached, and the creature lifted the goggles off its face to take a better look at me. It was Hewitt. He must have taken the goggles from Frank Goolz. Which meant that wherever Frank Goolz was, it wasn't a good place. And Suzie and Ilona were with him.

"Oh, cheese!" I yelped, spinning around to find an escape. "Oh, cheese, oh, cheese, oh, cheese!" I repeated, going as fast as I could toward the cemetery. I could hear the dogs barking and closing in. If Old Hewitt let go of the leash, I was done.

"Cheese, cheese, cheese!" I headed for the church. *Love sucks*, I thought as I slammed against the wall. I pushed myself off the chair, dropped onto the ground, and crawled into the hole like a mole on steroids. I wiped tears of fear out of my eyes and rolled over to pull my legs in after me. The dogs' noses poked excitedly into the hole, fighting to get in first. They yapped and barked as they scratched at the ground, digging to make the hole larger.

"Get, get, get!" Jonas Hewitt encouraged them.

I grabbed the jagged edge of the wooden floor and pulled myself up and in, scratching and tearing the skin on my stomach. I rolled onto my back.

"I'm dead," I said. Old Hewitt banged on the walls and howled. The dogs scratched the ground and barked. I tried to keep breathing as I grabbed a bench and struggled to push it over the hole. It only half covered it. It wouldn't keep them out for long. I crawled away from the hole and went for Alex's gun. I'd never fired a BB gun in my life. BBs would probably be like mosquito bites to dogs this size. I held it tight to my chest. I could hear the dogs snarling ravenously as they tried to tunnel into the church.

"GET! GET! GET!" Old Hewitt yelled. As far as I was concerned, I was pretty much gotten.

The bench I'd pushed over the hole shifted. It made little jumps as the dogs pushed against it. I pointed the BB gun and pulled the trigger, but nothing happened. I'd had recurring nightmares about being eaten by sharks that felt more comfortable than this. I held the BB gun by the barrel, thinking maybe I could use it as a bat against the first dog that came through the hole.

Old Hewitt threw something against the wall. From the sound of it, I knew it was my wheelchair. "I'm not weak like my boy. When I get you, I'll get you for good!" he shouted.

There was a plastic box glued to the butt of the gun. I opened it and BBs cascaded to the floor. I gathered them quickly, but now I had to figure out how to load them before the dogs got inside.

Outside, Old Hewitt started cursing at his dogs. I found a switch on the BB gun, pressed it, and cranked open the barrel. I tried to place a BB, but it fell on the floor because my hands were shaking so much. I finally managed to put one in place and push back the barrel. The dogs kept trying to twist their huge bodies through the hole. It was probably the first time in dog-attack history that the dogs were too big to do the job.

"Please help me," I said, holding the gun tightly against my chest.

"I'm going to kill you people, you hear!" Old Hewitt yelled, slamming his plank again and again against the wall.

"I hear," I whispered. The dogs had finally abandoned the hole and begun barking and scratching at the walls around the church. I heard Old Hewitt hammering at the chains and padlock at the main door.

My heart was trying to burst through my chest like a wild animal. I heard something move up by the ceiling. I looked up. A huge white owl peered down at me.

"If you stay around, you're going to see a real nice massacre," I told the owl. It seemed to nod. "Why don't you fly away like your mate? At least *you* can do that."

You'll have to learn to fly first. That was what Ilona had told me. I looked up at the owl, at the beam it was standing on, at the nest beside it.

There was something on the wall next to the nest: a trace, like a dark footprint, visible in a ray of moonlight. "You'll have to learn to fly first!" I shouted. "Sorry, owl." I aimed the gun, then took my chances and fired. The owl flew away. I missed the nest. I picked up one of the BBs that had fallen on the floor and reloaded the gun. This time I hit the nest, but it didn't budge. It was hopeless even if my theory was right. I reloaded the gun as the door started to crack under Old Hewitt's attack. I shot and hit the nest again. This time it moved a little. I searched the floor for another BB. Old Hewitt was kicking the door with all his might, and with each strike there were signs that he was almost in. The dogs knew it. They had stopped barking and were whining expectantly, ready to charge inside.

"We're gonna do you like we did that old witch!" Old Hewitt screamed, slamming his body against the door.

My finger found a BB on the floor. I put it into the barrel. Aimed.

"Please," I said, and shot. I hit the nest, but it barely moved.

"Crap, Ilona! Next time bury it!" I yelled. I thought it was the end of me, but the nest disagreed. A piece of it fell off. The rest stayed put, but it had gotten knocked off balance. A moment later the whole thing crashed to the floor with a THUD. I threw the gun aside and scrambled to the fallen nest like my life depended on it. And there it was. The Stone of the Dead.

I grabbed it and started turning the dials, praying for something to happen. The chain and the padlock were still holding the door. It had come open partway, but not enough to let them in. The dogs took turns poking their noses in. It sounded like they were barking my name.

"You're done getting into other people's business," Old Hewitt said, sliding the plank into the gap. He was using it as a lever to break the chain. I kept turning the dials on the Stone, crawling away from the door on my elbows as fast as I could. I reached the altar. There was nowhere else to go. The chain broke. The door flew open. The dials clicked. The Stone was jammed.

I looked up, bracing for an attack. But there were no dogs. Just reality rapidly expanding all around me. And then *POP!* The universe exploded in a maelstrom of light and sound. I closed my eyes. I heard Old Hewitt scream as loud as Peter had. The dogs yelped. And then there was silence.

The door was open wide, but I was alone inside the church, pressed against the wall by the altar, the Stone in my hand.

I knew something had changed. I felt it. This wasn't the reality I was used to. Even the feel of the air was different—colder, emptier, as if the church had moved outside the normal atmosphere and was drifting in space.

The light around me was too bright, even for a night with a huge full moon outside. The shadows of the benches went in the wrong direction, deep black lines toward the wide-open door. I looked up and saw a circle of white light right above me. Then, clutching the Stone desperately, I stood up. It seemed completely natural, like I had never been in a wheelchair. I was on my legs and it felt like something I did all the time. I could have walked out of the church. I decided to run. Not out of fear, out of pure joy. I was going as fast as I could when I jumped off the porch and landed on the cemetery grass.

"This is awesome!" I yelled. And then I saw the dogs. They were lying silently on their sides right outside the church. They didn't move. They didn't bark. They didn't even breathe. One second they were barking and yapping, ready to get me, and the next, they were lying there like three pelts of cold black fur.

Old Hewitt was nowhere to be seen. But I didn't want to stay around, in case he came back asking who killed his dogs. I had the feeling that losing the Stone would mean losing the use of my legs again, so I held it tight as I walked down the hill toward the Hewitt place. I was sure that's where I would find the Goolz.

21

DEAD
BOY
WALKING

had never seen the Hewitts' property before, and it
was as spooky as I'd expected. It stank something
horrible—like a mixture of wet dogs, gasoline, and
chicken poop. The ground was covered in sticky mud
dotted with wrecked cars, broken washing machines,
and rusted barrels. I walked past a refrigerator lying on
its side. The door had been removed and replaced with
wire mesh to create a pen for some scraggly rabbits. I
pulled my sweater up over my nose. It was no surprise
Alex and his dad were in horrible moods all the time. If
I had to live in that stench, I might go around hurting
people too.

"Ilona?" I called, still clutching the Stone. Most

of the buildings looked like animal barns, but past a dumpster, there was one that looked more like a human dwelling. There was an old rotting sofa on the porch and, above it, a bare light bulb surrounded by giant bugs.

"I don't like this," I told the Stone.

"Mr. Goolz?" I called, stepping onto the porch. "Are you in there?"

I leaned forward to listen at the door. I thought I heard knocks and voices, so I walked behind the rotten sofa and peered through a window into the kitchen. There was nothing there but a horrible mess of dirty dishes and trash. I moved to another window in a darker part of the house. But when I got close to the glass, I moved back in horror, nearly falling off the porch into the putrid mud. The figure reflected in the window was looking at me with two glassy white globes instead of eyes. I moved my hand. The reflection moved its hand, only it was all bones and skin and no flesh.

I looked down at my hands and they looked absolutely normal. I approached the glass to take a better look. Thanks to the Stone, I was walking again, but in my reflection I looked as dead as Madame Valentin. I looked like a monster.

"Am I dead?" I asked my zombie reflection. I set the Stone down on the floor like it was toxic and stared at myself in the window. I touched my face. I touched the empty eyes. I was the stuff of nightmares.

"Am I dead?" I asked the window again. I didn't want to be dead. I looked down at the Stone. "You did this to me!" I wanted to kick it away, but I heard a voice and looked back up at the window. Something was moving on the hallway floor. Or rather, the entire floor was moving—there was a trapdoor and somebody was trying to get out.

"Ilona!" I called. I skirted the sofa and opened the front door. "Ilona!"

"Harold! Down here!" she replied, banging on the trapdoor.

"Good boy!" Frank Goolz said.

"Get us out of here!" Suzie yelled, and the trapdoor moved up and down as someone pushed on it. It was secured with chains and a huge old padlock. I squatted to get a better look.

"Where's the key?" I asked.

"I think Hewitt has it. Where is he?" Ilona answered.

"His dogs are dead," I said, since that was the only information I had.

"Go into the kitchen," Frank Goolz said. "All my things are there. You can use the gun on the padlock."

I went into the kitchen. Frank Goolz's satchel was

217

there on the table, along with the revolver, his orange pad and pen, and my phone. I picked up the gun and went back to the trapdoor.

"You sure this thing isn't going to explode in my hand when I shoot?" I asked. It was extremely heavy and didn't feel safe at all.

"We'll soon know," Frank Goolz said.

I heard them scurrying down a flight of stairs—in case the revolver did explode, I suppose.

"Harold?" Frank Goolz called from far below.

"Yes?"

"Shoot the padlock. Now!"

I cocked the gun. It made an old metallic noise like a tin can being squeezed. I aimed at the padlock, looked away, and shot. It made an enormous *KABOOM* and the recoil knocked me onto the ground. I fanned the acrid smoke with a shaky hand and picked up the revolver from where I'd dropped it. It hadn't exploded, but neither had the padlock.

"Everybody all right down there?" I called.

"We're fine," Ilona said. "How's the padlock?"

"It's fine too," I said. "I'm going to shoot it again." I leaned down a little, bringing the barrel really close to the lock. I shot it at nearly point blank. *KABOOM.* It made an even greater noise, like a thousand metallic springs jumping out of a box, and the force of the shot vibrated up my arm. I fanned the smoke away with my hand and leaned down to check the padlock. "It worked!" I said. I struggled to free it from the chain.

"Don't shoot, I'm coming up," Ilona shouted.

"I'm not gonna shoot anymore." I set the gun on the ground and pushed it away from me.

I removed the chain, and Ilona pushed the trapdoor open so hard that I fell back on my butt.

"Oh, thank God, Harold," she said, and crawled over to hug me tight.

Then she pulled back, frowning. "Where's your chair?" she asked. "How did you get here?"

I waited for Frank Goolz and Suzie to come out and enjoy the show.

"You're not going to believe this," I said and tried to stand up. I failed. I tried again. I failed again. It was like waking up in the middle of a dream where you could fly.

I couldn't fly anymore.

"No," I said, looking up at them.

"What?" Suzie asked. Ilona looked at me with sad eyes.

"No, no, no," I repeated. "I need the Stone. I need it now!"

Ilona tried to touch my arm. "It's all right, Harold.

You're going to be all right."

I pushed her hand away. "I don't need your pity! I NEED THE STONE! GET IT FOR ME!"

Frank Goolz squatted in front of me. "We need to get out of here. I can carry you."

"I don't want to be carried. I want you to go outside, pick up the Stone on the porch, and bring it back to me." The more they looked at me, the more I hated myself. "You people are useless!" I screamed. I started to crawl toward the door to get the Stone back.

"Harold, stop," Ilona said.

"Leave me alone!" I didn't care how pathetic I sounded. All I wanted was to get the Stone back and turn it. Maybe I would look like a decomposing cadaver in every mirror for the rest of my life, but I didn't care.

"Harold!" she yelled. I didn't stop. I was nearly at the door when I realized she'd been trying to warn me. Hewitt was on the porch. Instead of his usual plank of wood, he was holding a shotgun. His face was covered in mud and bloody scratches. His clothes were torn. His expression was murderous. Wherever he had gone after setting the dogs on me at the church, it didn't look like it had been a picnic.

"You people," he said, aiming the shotgun at the Goolz. I looked over my shoulder. Frank Goolz had picked up his revolver and was pointing it at Hewitt.

"Or we could talk this through," Frank Goolz said.

"You brought her back," Hewitt said. "You brought her back from the dead."

"You killed her, right?" Frank Goolz asked. "All those years ago. You and Donahue killed her. That's why she came back and went after your kids."

"She's dead!" he yelled, tightening his grip on the shotgun. Clearly, he wanted to put an end to this discussion.

"If you tell me where you buried her body, I can help you find your son," Frank Goolz insisted. "He might be still alive."

"She got what she deserved!" he yelled, ignoring Frank Goolz's offer. "She's dead and in hell!"

"No, she's not," I said, looking past him. "She's here."

She was standing by the dilapidated fridge. She leaned over and tore off the mesh, freeing the rabbits. They jumped out of their prison and ran away in all directions. Old Hewitt turned around slowly, keeping his shotgun pointed at Frank Goolz. He screamed when he saw Madame Valentin staring at him with her empty white eyes.

"You're dead!" he screamed at her. "Go away!"

She didn't. Instead, she let go of the mesh and

walked toward him at a slow, even pace, her expression perfectly calm. He aimed his shotgun at her, but she didn't seem to care. She kept coming at him, even when he shot at her again and again, like she didn't belong in the same dimension as the bullets he was shooting.

"You killed my dogs!" Hewitt yelled. He kept shooting until he had no more ammunition. She stopped right in front of the porch, still looking very calm. He flung the shotgun at her. It bounced off like she was a wall, and she stepped up onto the porch. She was coming for him and he knew it.

"You're dead!" Hewitt cried. He fell to his knees. "Please go."

She stood right above him and cupped his chin with her half-skinned, mummified hand, her dark nails and bones pressing hard into his fat cheeks, forcing him to look into her eyes.

"I didn't kill you," he pleaded. "The dogs killed you. I didn't want them to kill you. I just wanted them to scare you off. Please, just leave me alone."

But she kept staring into his eyes until he started crying like a little boy. "We were dumb kids. It was an accident. We wanted to scare you off, that's all. It was an accident. I'm sorry. I'm sorry!"

She let go of his chin and he fell to the floor, curling up at her feet like a dying bug.

She looked down at me and smiled—I think. It was hard to say. With her mummified cadaver lips, she always seemed to be grinning. Then she walked over to the Stone of the Dead and picked it up. She cradled it against her chest with both hands and continued past us into the house. We watched her disappear into the darkness at the end of the hallway.

Old Hewitt was still curled up on the porch, sobbing. "It was the dogs. The dogs did it," he repeated.

"I think she's gone," Ilona said, bending to help me to sit up against the wall.

"She took the Stone with her," I said. I hadn't known she could do that.

Frank Goolz kept the revolver pointed at Hewitt, who was still sobbing. "Well, I guess we should wake up Officer Miller, then," he said.

"She took the Stone!" I repeated. I could feel tears welling up in my eyes. "Why did she do that?"

"I think she's taking it back to where it belongs, Harold," Frank Goolz said. "She's taking it back to hell."

22

THE
GOOLZ
NEXT DOOR

Old Hewitt confessed to two crimes: the accidental killing of Madame Valentin decades ago, when he and Donahue were kids and had set the dogs on her, and the recent murder of Donahue during a terrible fight on his boat.

They had been visited by Madame Valentin's ghost every night since Frank Goolz started playing with the Stone of the Dead. Donahue had been losing his mind over it, and was starting to think that the only way to stop her from haunting them was to confess. Old Hewitt disagreed, and they'd fought. It ended when Hewitt bashed in Donahue's skull with the plank of wood and dropped his body in the crab tank.

Old Hewitt led the police to an abandoned clay

mine, where they found the perfectly mummified remains of Madame Valentin. They also found Alex and Peter there, trapped with her body at the bottom of a deep pit.

"Oh, that must have been so uncomfortable," Suzie said, smiling. "Serves them right. Ha! Bullies!"

We were back in the tiny meeting room in the Newton police station. Officer Miller said that Mum was on the way, then he practically ran out of the room.

"She didn't want to kill them," Frank Goolz told us when we were alone. "She wanted people to look for the boys, and find her body in the process. Very clever!"

He also said that Madame Valentin, the Stone of the Dead, and I were connected in an unusual way. "I believe you are a very special boy, Harold," he said. "You have a marvelous gift for the ghostly. A talent for seeing past the shadows. It's a blessing."

He smiled, put his hand on my shoulder, and squeezed until it hurt. Somehow, though, it made me feel a little better about losing the Stone and all its magic.

"You'll be fine," Ilona told me, and I knew everything would be okay. That is, until I heard a tornado come into the station shouting my name. Mum had arrived.

• • •

"Mum!" I called. "Please?"

"No," she said from downstairs, where she was working on her next savory pie. Mum had reinstated the Goolz embargo and even said she would press charges if they dragged me into danger again.

"This is ridiculous," I told her, playing with the stair lift to annoy her with the noise. "The Goolz are heroes! You should want me to spend *more* time with them. Those two idiots would have died in that cave without them."

"You said they weren't idiots anymore."

Mum was right. After the dust had settled, Peter and Alex paid me a visit at home. But not to drag me to the beach and abandon me to the tide like they used to. They came to make peace and to thank me for playing a part in their rescue. They sat at our kitchen table, ate some of Mum's cheesecake, and listened to her jokes without mocking her accent. They even shook my hand before they left.

"You're awesome, English boy," Alex said. "Always thought so."

Spending time with a mummified cadaver had changed them deeply. Or maybe, now that the sins of their fathers had been brought to justice, in this world and the next, a magical grudge had been lifted from their shoulders, and they could become who they were really meant to be. Whatever it was, they were bullies no more.

• • •

"Please, Mum?" I said later, watching her weed the vegetable garden.

"No," she said.

I was on the porch. Ilona was sitting on the floor of her own porch on the other side of the bridge. We exchanged nods and brief waves when Mum wasn't looking.

"This sucks," I mouthed, hoping Ilona could read my lips.

She smiled and mouthed back, "I know!"

Her father had even built a ramp for me, waving and smiling at Mum as she stared at him incredulously.

When I turned back to Mum, she was on her knees, holding a bunch of vivid orange carrots, and watching our silent conversation.

"Why do you have to make me play the bad guy?" she asked.

"Please, Mum."

She briefly closed her eyes, then sighed and put her hands on her hips, trying to look all stern and authoritarian, which didn't really work when she was holding a bunch of carrots. "No more dangerous adventures!" she yelled.

My heart started to beat faster. I knew she was finally giving in.

"No more dangerous adventures!" I agreed, my voice coming out about two octaves too high.

She shook her head in disbelief and dropped the carrots into her vegetable basket. "I'm going to regret this."

"No, you won't," I said.

"Go on, then."

She didn't have to tell me twice. I was already flying down the path to the bridge.

"And Harold!" Mum called. "You go no farther than their house or yard, do you hear me?"

But I wasn't listening anymore. Ilona jumped off her porch and ran to the other side of the bridge. I crossed it without anyone's help and stopped in front of her, my wheels sinking into the sand.

"Your mum is watching us," she said, but she leaned over me and gave me a wonderful hug anyway. "I missed you, Harold Bell."

"I missed you, Ilona Goolz."

Mum was standing in the middle of our garden, holding her basket of vegetables. She wasn't angry anymore. She was sad. Or happy. Whatever she was, I knew she was trying not to cry at seeing me so happy to be back with Ilona. Mum and I gave each other a little nod. Then she turned her back and went into the house because she'd started to cry and didn't want me to see.

"Should we try the ramp?" Ilona asked. "Dad built it, so it might collapse."

It didn't.

Frank Goolz and Suzie were in the kitchen enjoying watery cocoa and horrible cookies when we came in.

"There's Harold!" Frank Goolz said. "Would you like some cocoa?"

I nodded, and Suzie made me a cup. Ilona handed me a cookie, and everything was right again.

"I was just on the phone with Officer Miller," Frank Goolz said. "Hewitt is talking like he's unloading a weight he's had on his shoulders for years."

Ilona sat beside me, then did something I didn't expect. She took my hand, right in front of her dad and sister. I looked at her. She smiled. Frank Goolz didn't seem to notice or care. He just wanted to tell his story.

"Killing Madame Valentin was sort of an accident, just like he told us," he said.

She had come to talk to Old Hewitt's parents because he and Donahue had beaten up a kid at school that day. But his parents weren't at home, and the boys unchained the dogs when they saw Madame Valentin walking down the road from the cemetery. They only wanted to scare her off. The dogs saw it differently and . . . well, you know what happened next. Then the boys got really scared and carried her body in a trolley to an abandoned mine in the marsh. They hid her body in a box deep in the mine and hoped they would get away with it.

"And they did," Frank Goolz said, "until we started using the Stone of the Dead, opening doors between this world and the next."

I was about to drink some of my bad cocoa when someone knocked on the open door. I turned around and saw two girls about Suzie's age standing on the porch. It was the Farrell twins, the daughters of a family that lived on the far edge of Bay Harbor. You could see their parents' farm from the road, right beside the Mallow Marsh. The Farrells were strange people. They homeschooled their daughters and were members of some kind of cult. The girls were dressed like they had just escaped a Gothic novel set in a time before hot water and electricity. One of them was carrying a shoebox.

"Can I help you?" Frank Goolz asked, standing up and walking to the door.

"We heard you found the missing boys," one of the sisters said.

"Our mother is missing. She's been missing a week," the other one continued.

Suzie, Ilona, and I joined them at the door.

"Missing? Is that right?" He frowned, but his eyes lit up.

"Isn't this something your dad should report to the police?" Ilona asked.

"Dad doesn't want to go to the police," one of them said.

"And we found this in the high grass by the marsh," said the other one, opening the box so we could all see what was in it. Inside the shoebox was a human foot severed at the ankle.

"Cheese! It stinks!" Ilona covered her nose.

"I don't like the sight of blood," Suzie said, turning pale.

"I just promised Mum we're not going on any more dangerous adventures!"

"Well, girls," Frank Goolz said, "let me get my satchel."

ACKNOWLEDGMENTS

Thanks to Ruben and Dulce Gerson for their unlimited love and support; to Maria Ahlund for her kindness and her Guns N' Roses brand of patience; to Jacques and Sylvie Flatin for their caring attention and counsel; to Melissa Bengorine for her camaraderie and all the fun she always delivers; to Thomas Leclere for his friendship and his enthusiasm for everything Goolz; to Franco and Trish Cook for all the inspirational talks and for being my very own Goolz Next Door; to Isabelle Perrin for her awesome work on this project and her strange taste for heart emojis; to Julia Morot and Manon Barbry for being my awesome friends; to Jola Kudela for taking the right picture at the right time; to Daphnée Colleau for always uplifting me; to Anaelle and Maena Rabaneda for their undivided attention to my silly jokes and being such efficient recipients of my love.

Thanks to my amazing agents, Ellen Levine and Alexa Stark, as well as Meredith Miller, at Trident Media Group, for their commitment and their wonderful work to support this project from the get-go.

And a very special thanks to Mary Colgan, and her team at Boyds Mills Press, for being the instrumental force, and one of the true talents behind The Goolz Next Door.

Born in Paris to an international family (one part
French, two parts Spanish, one part strange), Gary
Ghislain grew up between Paris and the French
Riviera. He now lives in Antibes on the French
Riviera with his two daughters, Ilo and Sisko,
enjoying the sun and the sea while working on his
novels. He is also the author of *How I Stole Johnny
Depp's Alien Girlfriend*. Visit garyghislain.blogspot.com.